"Toili"

WELSH LEGENDS

WELSH LEGENDS
and
FAIRY LORE

by

D. Parry-Jones

Illustrated by

Ivor Jones

BARNES
&NOBLE
BOOKS
NEW YORK

This Edition Published by Barnes & Noble Books, Inc.
by arrangement with B.T. Batsford, Ltd.

1997 Barnes & Noble Books

Printed and bound in the United States of America

ISBN 0-88029-996-7

97 98 99 00 01 M 9 8 7 6 5 4 3 2

QF

PREFACE

IN this volume the reader will find a fully representative collection of Welsh fairy lore and of the various classes of legends chosen. I need not remind anyone who is at all familiar with the vast choice at one's disposal that a large body of folk-lore, superstitions and legends has had to be omitted—a book of this prescribed size could not possibly include them all, even in their barest outline. It was a temptation to range lightly over this immense field, picking odd examples from here and there, but it was resisted in favour of my present choice, because it had advantages that more than compensated for the limitation, in that a much fuller treatment of the subjects could be given. If, of course, it arouses fresh interest in our general folk-lore, a further selection can be made in another volume.

Many of the stories given in this book may now only be found in rare books, and magazines—largely vernacular—which flourished in the early and middle decades of the last century and are therefore available only in our larger and central libraries. I mention this because I want to put on record my deep obligation especially to the National Library at Aberystwyth. With great indulgence they permitted returning dates to be extended time and again.

It is with pleasure, too—for the third time—that I express my gratitude to Dr. Noëlle Davies, for reading the proofs and for every kind help.

D. PARRY-JONES

CONTENTS

INTRODUCTION

IT is, unfortunately, rather late in the day now for writers on folk-lore to hope to get much more new material. Occasionally something comes along from an out-of-the-way corner of the country, and one may get a new twist to an old story. But since the art of story-telling, with the advent of other interests, has died out in the countryside, what one often gets is a curious hash, inextricably mixed up, of what was heard in early youth and hardly ever recalled since. The position is, however, not as bad as it would seem, for we are in possession of a vast and valuable collection, much of it contributed about the middle of the last century to the many popular magazines, notably *Y Brython* (1858–63). Mention ought also to be made of the local papers, and a tribute paid to the enlightened men who edited them, men who were always willing to put a column at the disposal of a countryman with a legend, a story, or a bit of folk-lore to tell.

There may be yet something hidden away in the home of a secretary of an early *Eisteddfod*, or in the possession of his children, or grandchildren—which I am afraid is now equivalent to being lost! It was a great pity that no attempt was made to co-ordinate these small cultural efforts on a district or county basis, and some supervision exercised by a central body over the material contributed. Much interesting matter has, I am afraid, been lost for ever. The position is very little better today.

I determined at the very outset to tell the stories and legends in full, always reserving to myself the right—often used—of cutting out vague and waste verbiage, which obscured the outline of the story and clogged its movement. I am convinced that the average reader wants to have the legends and stories as they were told round the fireplaces of Wales in the hey-day of story-telling.

I have already referred to our great debt to the vernacular magazines, the weekly papers and the local *eisteddfodau* for the preservation of the majority of our legends and folk-lore. These were for the most part contributed by country folk who were content merely to record the versions prevalent in their districts—folk who possessed neither the qualifications nor the desire to classify them or enlarge upon their origin, character, or significance. But towards the end of the century there appeared on the scene more scholarly men, like Wirt Sikes, Elias Owen and, especially, Sir John Rhys who stood—and still stands—in a class of his own. Sir John was a Welshman from the Welsh countryside, a Celtic scholar of acknowledged eminence and one profoundly interested in all aspects of Welsh life, not least its superstition, folk-lore and mythology. At almost every turn the Welsh student of today labours under a deep debt of gratitude to him, and I want here to acknowledge my indebtedness to him in this particular field.

Under "Bibliography" I have given a list of the books and periodicals that I made use of. A large number of those in the vernacular are now scarce but are still available through libraries.

Sir John expresses his regret that he did not start to collect the lore and legends of his country much earlier; for this lack of early interest he can only blame—and justly—the old-time schoolmaster, and the ideas under which he laboured, prominent amongst them the idea that a school dealt with nothing but what was to be found in books. Such things as legends, folk-stories and superstitions were best left to the peasant, to occupy and interest the minds of those who had had no education. He was the last systematic collector, and it is our great good fortune that he started when he did, for he was still in time—the seventies and eighties of the last century—to meet old people who had heard their stories from other old people. When an old man of 80 or more tells his tales as heard in early youth from men equally old, a period of nearly a century and a half is spanned, and one is back in the early decades of the eighteenth century. And Wales did not lose much in the way of communal games, national customs, habits of life, lore and legend for another hundred years. By that time Methodism had become such a power in the land that these things, even where they were not directly attacked, began to die out, and a new Wales emerged in which religion, the respectability that went with it, the striving to "get on," and the pursuit of culture became the main concerns of the people. Not only were the old lore and customs held to be unworthy of an emancipated and enlightened age, but they were condemned as belonging to a past that was ignorant and superstitious and in bondage to sin. They were contrary to the teaching of the gospel which gave no place in its system to the existence of fairies, goblins or ghosts, only to the devil and his wicked angels.

Sir John tells us that he had the utmost difficulty in getting people to talk to him about fairies and such matters at all. It was only the fact that he was a Welsh-speaking Welshman and a scholar of such repute that helped them to overcome their sense of shame even to confess that they had ever heard them. An opening that he found generally successful was to tell a story himself and then to ask them if they had heard anything like it. The interest of so great a man in the subject cast some dignity over it, and was invariably enough to thaw frozen tongues; even then a request was made not to mention their names. I understand very well the reticence of these old people; they knew the previous age and were proud and grateful to think that they were emancipated from all superstition, and that higher and better things now occupied their minds.

T. Gwynn Jones, in his *Welsh Folklore*, says: "My own father used to tell stories and sing songs for us when we were very young, but later, having come under the influence of the religious activities of the time, he gave up the practice, considering it to be sinful. When later I became interested in Folklore and prayed him to repeat for me some of his former stories and songs, he refused to comply. Thus, throughout the district, a mass of such material was for ever lost."

Marie Trevelyan, in *Folk-lore and Folk-stories of Wales*, says: "For various reasons—chiefly religious—the names of persons . . . have not been mentioned." "C.D. These initials indicate an old inhabitant (whose) surviving relatives have religious reasons for desiring anonymity"!

In view of this it is curious to note that by common consent a traditional licence was granted to an old and secular institution— the *eisteddfod*—to extend its interest and patronage to these things and to offer prizes for the best collection of ballads, local folk-lore and superstition, matters that were regarded as within its legitimate sphere, and part of its function to foster. And a man would be tempted to compete in one of these items who on other occasions would not avow his interest in them. This venerable institution had retained a place in the mind of the people high enough to throw a mantle of dignity over such studies as these, and it is to such competitions at our many *eisteddfodau*, large and small, that we owe not a few valuable collections.

It is possibly a good thing for us that these stories were collected and put in print before our collectors became acquainted with— and, perhaps, deterred by—such things as Comparative Folk-lore, or the Science of Mythology; they were entirely free from any pre-conceived notions and ranged widely over the field, putting down everything exactly as they heard it, asking no questions as to whether it conformed to any pattern or fitted into any classification. They possessed no formula by reference to which they might reject a story in part or *in toto* as being inconsistent with its strict requirements. It would have made our task easier in some cases had they rejected a few made up of bits from different stories—possibly the confused mixture of some "grey old man of the corner," whose memory was beginning to fail him, or the contribution of one who had only heard them in a truncated and mutilated form.

INTRODUCTION

I do not wish my remarks to be taken as in any way a disparagement of the scholarly works of those people who have applied their vast knowledge to the study and classification of our folklore and folk-stories, bringing thereby order into the chaotic mass that we have inherited, and throwing so much light on the working of the primitive mind.

Wirt Sikes, in his book *British Goblins*, is inclined, I think, to make too elaborate a classification, though at the same time he has to admit that "it is not possible to classify them by fixed and immutable rules . . . the writer can only govern himself by the purpose of orderly arrangement." After all, it must be borne in mind that these stories were a part of the lore of peasant folk who were not capable of drawing fine distinctions between the various orders of non-human beings and spirits. I very much doubt whether the countrymen of West Wales amongst whom I was brought up would be able to distinguish between *Ellyllon*, "the pigmy elves who haunt the groves and valleys and correspond pretty closely with the English elves," and *Ellydan*, "a species of elf exactly corresponding to the English Will-o'-wisp." These seem to me to be dictionary names, rather than names taken from the living vocabulary in popular use by the countryman. Elias Owen, in *Welsh Folk-lore*, says that originally *Tylwyth Teg* and *Ellyll* were terms used to describe "two different kinds of beings, but in the course of time the words became interchangeable, and thus their distinctive character was lost. In English the words fairies and elves are used without any distinction."

The ordinary countryman knew of

FAIRIES and GHOSTS

BWCIOD.   A comprehensive term which included spirits and apparitions of any kind—imps, *gwr-drwgiaid*, or little devils, such as were called to their assistance by conjurors.

GWRACH-Y-RHIBYN.   Though sometimes referred to in masculine terms, *gwelwyd e'n y plwydd filoedd o weithe* (he was seen in the parish thousands of times), she would appear to be a female who showed herself before a death or some misfortune or other; and had a liking for sharp bends in the roads or paths. At the sight of water, or when crossing water, she uttered the most horrible shrieks. D. E. Jenkins, in *Beddgelert*, describes her as a female "of immense size and of an extremely hideous appearance. She had bright red hair, as coarse as a horse's tail . . . her two cheek-bones projected like two ridges and her curved nose reached almost to her pointed chin. Her eyes flashed red fire from their deep sockets." As she howled she showed two or three teeth "like the spikes of a harrow, lying one across the other."

TOILI, or spectral funeral. These were sometimes seen during the day, but more often at night and would seem to be made up of the phantom figures or spirits of the people who would actually be present at the funeral of which the TOILI was a portent—and a pre-view. It was only people possessing second sight who could see them in the day-time; these have been known to name every person in the procession and to say what each wore. These phantom figures would appear to have substance and mass, for a person who unwittingly became entangled in a spectral funeral usually found himself carried along with it until the crush eased a bit as they reached the churchyard gate. Many have been forced to accompany it for miles. In the night it was often seen preceded by a CANWYLL GORPH, a corpse-candle. "Sometimes the light was seen carried by a spectral representation of the dying person." But as a rule the *candle* was seen moving on its own.

CYHYRAETH. Another death portent. J. Ceredig Davies says that "this spirit was never seen, only its sound was heard." One may therefore be prepared to have varied and confused descriptions of it; indeed, from some accounts it would appear that it was not sharply distinguished from *gwrach-y-rhibyn*, and was another name for it. But from the more concise accounts it is plain that it was a separate spectre, having a *modus operandi* of its own. It was said to moan in the night before a death and its voice to resemble the groans of the sick person about to die. "It is heard passing through the empty streets and lanes by night, groaning dismally, sometimes rattling the window shutters, or flinging open the door as it flies by."

Speaking generally of West Wales, these were the personnel of the spirit world which could be described in the physical terms of human beings.

Though inclined in my opinion to over-elaboration, *British Goblins* is nevertheless a most valuable collection. It would have been more valuable still had the author seen fit to give us in all instances the sources of his information.

I have reserved the right of telling the stories in my own way, which meant keeping an eye on the oldest versions, choosing the ones that had been the least tampered with, and which gave the story in the most vivid manner. Telling them in my own way meant, when translating from the vernacular, stripping them of the florid multi-syllabic language—of *Glasynys*, for example—with which they were adorned, but which only served to retard their movement and blur their outline. Readers who are familiar with his version of the story of Elidorus, given by Giraldus Cambrensis, will not cease to hold him suspect for the liberties he took with it and for his version of many another; though Sir John Rhys does not think that he went so far as to add to any of them incidents of his own creation.

But then something may be said in extenuation of his treatment of them: The Wales of his age required something more than a mere fairy story—to be acceptable to both editor and reader it had to be made to teach a lesson and point a moral. It was not told simply because of its interest as a fairy story but quite as much because it lent itself readily as a vehicle to convey a moral lesson, and one will find at the end a long paragraph devoted to moralising and sermonising. "The Welsh always, in their popular tales, conclude with moral or prudential references."

In this enlarged and homilectic form they were made acceptable to the reading public of that age—the mid-Victorian—and may be said to fill the need supplied today by our short story. Fairy stories and novels were looked askance upon, and in the average home were not permitted to be read; some means had, therefore, to be found to overcome this prejudice. In the case of the novels of Daniel Owen it was discovered that to call them biographies rendered them innocuous and acceptable, and in this guise they were sent out to the public.

INTRODUCTION

In telling a story, some latitude ought to be given to those who possess a sense of the dramatic, the gift to tell it vividly and the power to put colour and life into it. Often they are dry bones lying along the valley and need to be clothed with flesh and have the breath of life breathed into their nostrils. The fact that more than one version of some of our legends was discovered in the countryside goes to show that in the hands of a story-teller of an inventive turn of mind it was impossible but that he should leave upon them the stamp of his art and genius. Even our famous collection—the *Mabinogion*—grew in the hands of successive tellers until they assumed the form in which we have them today.

Wales has from the earliest times had its order of bards and story-tellers moving from *Llys* (court) to *Llys* entertaining the princes and nobles with their friends and households.

A collection that may well stand as a pattern of how the problem should be approached is that of Hugh Evans, *Y Tylwyth Teg* (The Fairies), *Gwasg y Brython*. He set about his task, he tells us, with a well-defined purpose in his mind, and that was to tell the stories as he imagined they would be told originally by the old fathers who believed in them. That must have presented its own peculiar difficulties, but judging from his presentation of them, it meant cutting out dead wood and reducing the size of those swollen by the florid verbosity of Welsh Victorian writers.

The last native collector of ghost and fairy stories in Wales, who at the same time really believed in them, was the Reverend Edmund Jones (1702–93), an Independent minister of The Tranch, by Pontypool, Monmouthshire. He was not actuated by any of the motives of a modern folklorist, but was solely interested in them and their appearances as affording proof of the existence of orders of spiritual beings and of the immortality of the soul: "But some may yet enquire what may be the end and design of amassing together accounts of this nature, and making them publick? . . . It is designed to prevent a kind of infidelity which seems to spread much in the kingdom . . . [and] which hath a tendency to irreligion and atheism; for when men come to deny the being of *spirits*, the next step is to deny the being of God who is a *spirit* and the father of *spirits*." Those who speak against the

8

accounts of spirits and apparitions "are chiefly women, and men of weak womanish understanding . . . which cannot bear to be disturbed with what is strange and disagreeable to a pleasant vain mind." Thus the author, in a small volume published at Newport in 1813, but of which two previous editions had appeared, printed at Trevecca in 1767 and 1780. It bears a long title: *A Relation of Apparitions of Spirits, in the County of Monmouth, and the Principality of Wales, etc.* Immense changes have come over the minds of men since, and, by an irony of fate, the Reverend Edmund Jones is remembered today not for the work to which he devoted his life—the preaching of the gospel and the saving of souls—but for a minor activity which he accounted of little value except in so far as it aided him in his major task. As a preacher of the gospel he is long dead and forgotten, but as a collector of ghost and fairy stories his memory has survived, and his name is held in much affection for his enthusiasm and valuable records.

Great scholars have exercised their minds as to what may have been the origin of the belief in fairies, which are an order of beings quite separate from ghosts and goblins and similar apparitions. They shared much of the normal life of human beings: they ate, they drank, they married and were given in marriage and brought up families; yet they were a semi-spiritual race and were not in all things subject to terrestrial laws as man is. In some of the stories, high moral sentiments are attributed to them; nasty tricks, and senseless, even pitiless, conduct have been attributed to them in others, but this may be due to the fact that they have often been confused in the peasant mind with conjurors' devils and such-like creatures. It was only to be expected that legend should have had a say in the matter of their origin: "The Welsh have a very beautiful tradition to show how they came into being: When our Saviour was upon earth, there lived a woman who had a great many children. . . . Once she saw our Blessed Lord coming towards her house, and by some unaccountable impulse hid half her children so that Jesus Christ should not see them. When he had departed from her dwelling the mother went to look for the children . . . and found they had disappeared and she never saw them again. The children became the first fairies."

INTRODUCTION

Filial affection would prompt the living to try to probe into the mystery of the after-life and to inquire into the possible fate of their parents and ancestors. It was widely held that fairies were the spirits of folk who had died in a state not good enough for heaven nor yet bad enough for hell.

Anthropologists and students of primitive folk-lore have found attraction in the theory that these small people, defenceless, harmless and peaceful, possessing no weapons of war, having their homes in the woods, on the moors or in underground regions, and coming out only at night, might have been the first inhabitants of our island and driven to this mode of life by their conquerors. So fairies may well have their origin in historic fact. Many things in fairy lore seem to lend support to this theory: the fact, for example, that they buy in markets without uttering a word, which is taken to indicate that they were unfamiliar with the language of those around them. In some of the stories they are said to speak in a strange tongue. The further fact that their habitations are always represented as being in caves and underground regions, in wastes and inaccessible moors, agrees with what must have been the sad lot of the early inhabitants whose richer lands were taken from them by their stronger and more virile conquerors. From their horror of iron and of being touched by iron, it is surmised that it may have been the instrument of their conquest.

Then again they are often pictured as being poor and badly housed, coming out at night secretly to the houses of their wealthier neighbours, grateful for shelter and warmth to bath their babies by the fire. They came for the loan of simple and very ordinary household utensils, such as those used in baking, which in their primitive state of civilisation they did not possess. There is a whole cycle of stories which tells of their coming to fetch human midwives to assist at births, an admission of their more advanced knowledge. Their objection to the tilling of the soil and especially to the turning over of their green dancing rings, have also been noted, as indicating a very primitive state of existence. Mention has been made of their borrowing baking utensils, but had they advanced to that stage where they could bake bread, unless some of them were making efforts to emulate their more advanced neighbours? Giraldus Cambrensis says that they lived on "milk diet, made up into messes with saffron." To the fairy lady of *Llyn y Fan Fach*, the young suitor's bread seemed "crimped or overbaked: possibly the backward civilisation, to which she was supposed to belong, was content to support itself ... on a fare which included nothing deserving to be called bread at all ... the nearest approach to it being something of the consistency of porridge." Marriage by capture of women of this defenceless race may also point to a primitive age and to the natural conduct of an arrogant, conquering race.

A great deal more could be ranged in support of the theory that some of the fairy stories point to a "clash of races, and we may regard many of the fairy sagas as stories told by men of the Iron Age of events which happened to men of the Bronze Age in their conflicts with the men of the Neolithic Age." Still we must leave a large field for the exercise of man's imagination and fancy, though imagination has generally something to work upon, however flimsy.

A word about grouping. Satisfactory grouping of the legends and stories was a task that provided some difficulty. I was hoping to break away if possible from the usual—and did try—but I am not at all satisfied with my attempt. In most cases the legends centre round certain objects like wells, caves, lakes, etc., and one soon discovered that, even though it were possible, it was unwise to disturb unduly a classification that had been found happy and natural, if not inevitable.

The reader will discover that whole groups of subjects have been left out, due entirely to the prescribed size of the book: stories of ghosts, witches, wizards, weather lore, divination charms, folk-healing, encounters with the devil; stories from the *Mabinogion* and from the works of Giraldus Cambrensis, etc. King Arthur does figure in some of the stories, an older and less attractive hero, not yet the perfect mirror of chivalry that he later became.

Chapter One

FAIRY LORE—GENERAL

Yr hen ŵr llwyd o'r cornel   The grey old man of the corner
Gan ei dad a glywodd chwedel,   Of his father heard a story,
A chan ei dad fe glywodd yntau,   Which from his father he had heard
Ac ar ei ôl mi gofiais innau.   And after them I have remembered.

BEFORE I proceed to give any of the fairy stories, it will be well, I think, to give a brief description of them as they existed in the popular mind. On the whole it will be found that the stories present us with a fairly uniform picture of fairy life and activity. There are, of course, baffling inconsistencies due mainly to the fact that the peasant has at times confused fairies with ghosts, witches and spirits. But it is sufficient evidence of their uniform character when I say that had the story told by Giraldus Cambrensis at the end of the twelfth century come to light for the first time in Cardiganshire at the end of the nineteenth, the folklorist would have received it without lifting an eyebrow, as fitting naturally into the vast collection that is in our possession today.

The fairies were little folk of the size of children; their height has been given as about 2 feet. It will be seen later that there were bigger fairies, a thing not to be wondered at as there are small and big races amongst human beings—the Nordic and the Zulu being conspicuous for their height. The fairies of the Pennant neighbourhood in Caernarvonshire were said to be taller than the others and had light or even flaxen hair, with clear blue eyes, nor would they allow a person of dark complexion to come near them. But the typical fairy was a small creature. They were bright, cheerful, handsome and charming beings, with rosy cheeks, snow-white complexion and a mass of luxuriant, fair, curly hair falling in ringlets over their shoulders. They were lively in their action, fleet of foot, of a friendly disposition, "treating mortals with honesty and kindness." They were dressed most elegantly in white flowing robes with long trains—at least, the women— and when they danced they took hold of one another's trains and swept round the rings in perfect circles. Pembrokeshire fairies wore red, with red caps, and were at times mistaken for soldiers; indeed they were known there as "the folks of the red coats."

Cardiganshire fairies preferred green, which would seem to be the colour more popularly associated with them, though in parts of North Wales they were seen dressed in "blue petticoats."

The menfolk of this handsome little race were not a bit dress-conscious, and, unlike their womenfolk, were content to wear the familiar dark, home-spun clothes of the Welsh countryman of the last and previous centuries, including knee-breeches!

They are almost uniformly described as being of a friendly nature, grateful for every help given them in their difficulties, and kind to old people and those in need. Many such have received regularly silver coins for a long time, indeed, as long as they kept the secret to themselves, but once they advertised the fact, help immediately ceased, for the fairies were a shy and reserved folk and hated publicity. Especially did they appreciate the kindness of those who, before they went to bed, left them a clean, warm hearth, with plenty of water in a suitable vessel, to come at night and bath their babies there. Never did they depart without leaving on the table a piece of silver money.

There is a story told of a miller in North Wales, Robert Francis, that at the time of the year when he was drying corn he

Fairy Bathing in the Mill

used often to stay up late at night to attend to the fire, as a constant heat was essential. He made, therefore, frequent visits to the mill even past midnight. One night he happened to leave there a large vessel full of water, and on visiting the mill just before retiring he was surprised to see two little people there whom he took to be man and wife busily having a bath. Being a kind-hearted man and not wishing to disturb them, he went back and told his wife. "Oh," she said, "they are the fairies." After the lapse of some time he returned to the mill, but they were gone; they had, however, left the place perfectly clean and in good order, and in addition had left behind them a sum of money. This was not the end, they came again—and brought their friends with them—for the miller had now decided to leave that bathful of water there every night. As their number increased, so did the sum of money left behind. This went on for a long time to the mutual advantage of both parties, until one day the miller was foolish enough to tell his neighbours all about it. At once their visits and the money ceased. One invariable condition of their help and friendship was absolute secrecy. Similar tales of their gratitude and generosity can be matched from every part of Wales.

Their sole occupation—apart from bathing babies—seems to have been dancing, though their menfolk were occasionally seen hunting, and riding about on horses, "of the size of valley hares." Their womenfolk, too, have been seen riding about in fine carriages drawn by horses richly caparisoned. But what they liked doing most of all was dancing, especially on nights when the moon was full. Their fairy rings could be seen on practically all farms a hundred years ago, varying in size from comparatively small ones of seven yards across to those of three-quarters of an acre in size. They were often to be found under a big tree—a yew, oak or sycamore tree—but never a rowan tree, of which we shall hear a great deal later on. No cattle, except the Welsh mountain sheep, would graze in these circles, a fact that has been advanced to account for the superiority of Welsh mutton! Farmers maintained that when cultivated, fairy rings produced three times the crop of the land around, but it was a very dangerous thing to do, for it at once roused the ire of the fairies, and no farmer wished to have a tribe of angry fairies round him.

They came out of their habitations towards evening and the setting sun, showing preference for an evening with a little mist. As this spread itself out lightly and crept up the slopes they danced their way up in it; when it was very thick, only their heads could be seen bobbing up and down. Very old people declared that as children they often went out to watch them. The fairies were always accompanied by their musicians, who filled the air with their sweet and enchanting music, and so right through the night, until cock-crow, or sunrise, they tripped and carolled.

> From grasses bright, and bracken light,
> Come, sweet companions, come,
> The full moon shines, the sun declines,
> We'll spend the night in fun;
> With playful mirth, we'll trip the earth,
> To meadows green let's go.
> We're full of joy, without alloy,
> Which mortals may not know.

> O'r glaswellt glân a'r rhedyn mân,
> Gyfeillion dyddan dewch,
> E ddarfu'r nawn-mae'r lloer yn llawn,
> Y nos yn gyflawn gewch;
> O'r chwarau sydd ar dwyn y dydd,
> I'r dolydd awn ar daith,
> Nyni sydd lon, ni chaiff gerbron,
> Farwolion ran o'n gwaith.

And what a night they would have, especially if a mortal being —despite the words of the song—had unwittingly strayed into their circle, for nothing apparently pleased them better. In the morning these rings were often found to be quite bare, for such was "the vigour with which their tiny feet had capered on them."

Their habitations were universally believed to be underground, in dimly lit regions, with the entrance to them under a sod, near one of their circles, by some ancient standing stone, under the bank of a river, away on the open moor hidden by bushes, or in the ruins of an old castle, as on *Ynys Geinon* rock. In the midst of this castle there was a pit with a three-ton stone lying across it, and when they wanted ingress or egress, they uttered a secret word, and lo! the stone lifted, and fell back again of its own accord. From the entrance down to the underground passage they descended along a ladder of twenty-one or -two gold rungs.

Indeed, their abode might be right under the foundation of one's own house. A quaint and amusing, if pathetic, little story comes from Aberdaron in North Wales:

In a farm nearby there lived a farmer whose habit it was, before he retired for the night, to go a few steps outside the front door; indeed, it was the only door the house possessed, as was the case, then, in most farmhouses and cottages. While he was outside, this particular night, a stranger came up to him and in effect said: "My dear sir, you have no idea the great annoyance you cause me and my family like this every night." The farmer inquired how that could be, to which the stranger replied "that his house was just below where they stood, and if he would only stand on his foot he would see that what he said was true." The farmer did so and at once was able to see "that all the slops from his house" went down the chimney of the little fairy dwelling "which stood far below in a street that he had never seen before." He was then asked by the fairy if he wouldn't mind removing the door from the front to the back, promising him that if he did so his cattle would be ever clear of the disease called *clwy byr*—the black-quarter. The farmer, being a kind and considerate person, and fully realising what it all meant to the little family down below, consented to do so. The front door was blocked up and another opened at the back. After that the farmer became the most prosperous rearer of stock in that part of the country. "To place the whole thing beyond the possibility of doubt, Evan Williams (the smith) assured me that he had often seen the farmer's house with the front in the back."

"In the mountains near Brecknock there is a small lake (and) ... in ancient times, it is said, a door in a rock near this lake was found open upon a certain day every year, I think it was May day. Those who had the curiosity and resolution to enter, were conducted by a secret passage, which terminated in a small island, in the centre of the lake. Here the visitors were surprised with the prospect of a most enchanting garden, stored with the choicest fruits and flowers, and inhabited by the *Tylwyth Teg*, or *fair family*, a kind of fairies." Nothing could be seen by those who stood on the margin of the lake, "only an indistinct mass," but strains of soft music floated occasionally to the outside world, very likely when guests were being entertained, for the fairies were not only very beautiful, but extremely kind and courteous *to those who pleased them*, giving them gifts of fruits and flowers. One condition they made: Nothing was to be taken away.

On one occasion "a sacrilegious wretch" put a flower presented to him in his pocket, but "as soon as he touched unhallowed ground" outside, "the flower vanished and he lost his senses." At the time, they pretended to take no notice of it, but dismissed their guests with the usual courtesy and closed the door. "But their resentment ran high," and though they are undoubtedly still in this fragrant garden, the door has never been reopened, nor, indeed, seen. "From the date of this sacrilegious act, the *Cymry* have been unfortunate."

Though there is a surprising unanimity in assigning their abode to underground regions, yet in Pembrokeshire they were said to inhabit certain green isles out at sea to the west of St. Davids, islands which at times could be seen rising through the mist, and on which, without their realising they were fairy islands, sailors have before now landed. These were supposed to be connected with the mainland by subterranean passages, along which the fairies came to do their shopping in the markets of Haverfordwest and other places along the southern coast of Pembrokeshire. They favoured certain tradesmen—being especially partial to one particular butcher in Milford Haven—who may have got used to them and their ways, for they said not a word but "bought in silence their meat and other necessaries, and leaving the money (generally silver pennies), departed, as if knowing what they would have been charged. They sometimes were visible and at other times invisible." Yet folk knew of their presence, for the price of things went up.

Gwynionydd, a native of Cardiganshire, gives an account of the fairies (*Plant Rhys Ddwfn*, as they are called in some parts of South Wales) and the region they inhabited, which agrees somewhat with the location of the green islands in that it is to the west of the Pembrokeshire coast. "There is a tale current in *Dyfed* (Pembrokeshire) that there is, or rather there has been, a country between Cemmes, the northern hundred of Pembrokeshire, and Aberdaron in Lleyn. The chief patriarch of the inhabitants was *Rhys Ddwfn*, and his descendants used to be called after him the children of *Rhys Ddwfn*. They were, it is said, a handsome race enough, but remarkably small in size. It is stated that certain herbs of a strange nature grew in their land, so that they were able to keep their country from being seen . . . herbs [that] grew . . . on a small spot about a square yard in area in a certain part of Cemmes. If it chanced that a man stood alone on it, he beheld the whole of the territory of *Plant Rhys Ddwfn*; but the moment he moved he would lose sight of it altogether. . . . In another story the requisite platform was a turf from St. David's churchyard."

They were apparently engaged in no occupation, did not practise agriculture, had no schools or any kind of learning, and could not, it would seem, count beyond five, an inference based on the account of the fairy of *Llyn y Fan Fach*, who counted her cattle in fives. Support is also lent to this theory by an old Welsh air "*Clychau Aberdovey*" which is said to have originally had only *un, dau, tri, pedwar, pump*—one, two, three, four, five—the six and seven being later added to meet the arbitrary demands of a new musical arrangement.

Their general intelligence and mental perception fell far below that of human beings and they could easily be imposed upon and outwitted. There is a story, taken by Wirt Sikes from *The Principality*, which tells of *Dewi Dal*, a farmer, whose home became so overrun with fairies that he could not sleep at night for the row they made. He consulted the wise man who advised him, as it was the time to cut the corn in the big field (*cae mawr*) which was a day's work for fifteen reapers, to ask his wife to say aloud, "I will prepare food for fifteen men who are going to mow the *Cae Mawr* tomorrow," to which Dewi was to reply—again aloud—"Yes, do, and see that the food is substantial and sufficient." His wife assured him that the men should have enough. "They shall be fed according to our means." She then set about to prepare this "substantial and sufficient" meal: first of all she caught a sparrow, feathered and trussed it and roasted it like a fowl before the kitchen fire. After that she "placed some salt in a nutshell, and set the sparrow and the salt, with a small piece of bread, upon the table ready for fifteen men." When the fairies saw the size of the meal prepared for so many hefty outdoor workers, they said to one another, "Let us quickly depart from this place, for alas, the means of our hosts are exhausted. Who before this was so (poor) . . . as to serve up a sparrow for . . . fifteen men?" They left that very night and Dewi and his family had peace.

Fairies were universally held to be clean folk, who valued nothing better than to have a well-swept, tidy hearth to come to at night—if, in addition, a clean cloth was laid on the table with a little bread and milk left on it, and the provision of a panful of water in which they could wash, they were highly delighted. Knives had, of course, to be hidden away. Then in the morning the kind maids, especially the clean ones, would find lying about somewhere, often in their shoes, a very acceptable silver coin. Sometimes the money would be in fairy currency, resembling the petals of flowers, which upon being taken up crumbled into dust. Nevertheless, they liked to get it, for it was supposed to bring luck. Lazy and slovenly maids who went to bed leaving their kitchens untidy and in disorder they could not abide; they would enter the bedrooms of such at night and pinch them until they reformed themselves, singing the following song while they were thus engaged:

> "We're fond of truth and cleanliness,
> And all clean folks we'll always bless;
> But O! the nasty dirty jade
> Shall for her filthiness be paid.

> Chorus: Come pinch her, pinch her, pinch away,
>   Black, purple, yellow, pinch away."

They were credited with the possession of certain supernatural gifts and knew what passed between persons spoken outside their houses, but not what was said inside. They appeared oftener to men than to women, and to uneven numbers, one, three, five, etc., oftener than to groups of even numbers. Less cautious, for some reason, on Fridays than on other days, they were consequently more often seen on that day, generally having one bigger than the rest going before them. They were believed in some parts to spend seven years upon earth, seven underground and seven in the air.

There are stories of wicked fairies, some with the nasty habit of thieving, but on the whole they are spoken of as being honest folk in their dealings with human beings, generously responsive to any considerate treatment. This is an old belief, for Giraldus Cambrensis tells us that they "never took an oath, for they detested nothing so much as lies. . . . They reprobated our ambition, infidelities and inconsistencies; they had no form of public worship, being strict lovers and reverers, as it seemed of truth."

Not only did they try to reform slovenly maids, but they endeavoured to do good to the families of their neighbourhood, being especially concerned to teach them "to keep all promises and covenants to which they pledged themselves": In upper Arllechwedd, in Arfon, there was a brute of a husband who constantly ill-treated his wife. One day they took the matter in hand, and while the two were out ploughing in the field, the wife leading the team, something went wrong and he visited his ill-temper and annoyance upon her. "No sooner had he done so, than he was snatched through the air and plunged into" *Corwrion* lake. When the poor woman went to the lake to plead for his return, the only answer she had was that in the lake he was and in the lake he should remain—as much as to say, it is the best place for such brutes.

Having no religion, or any form of divine worship, it is not surprising to be told that, again in the neighbourhood of the above lake, they were often seen mowing their hay on Sundays.

As to what their general attitude towards the Christian religion was there is very little evidence to go by, but there are one or two bits which show that it was hostile. In Cardiganshire it was firmly believed that one class of them were definitely hostile and particularly so to the Methodists, whom they had singled out for their especial disfavour, going so far on one or two occasions as to molest visiting ministers. But, here, the peasantry may have confused the fairies with another order of supernatural beings, though one writer says that he had been informed by a Monmouthshire person "that they are not partial at all to the gospel and that they left Monmouthshire on account of there being so much preaching, praying to, and praising God, which were averse to their dispositions." The old guide to the waterfalls of Glyn Neath also said the same thing, that is, that they were driven away from *Craig y Dinas* "by the preaching of the gospel."

It is rather difficult to reconcile this attitude with the general character of kindliness and goodwill attributed to them and the known zeal with which some of them pursued their mission of fostering friendliness and good neighbourhood amongst humans. For in their self-appointed task they adopted various disguises and entered certain cottages "in order to ascertain the extent of the people's kindness."

One evening they visited the home of *Morgan ap Rhys* in the region of Cader Idris. Morgan was at home before his fireplace and in a very good mood enjoying "his pipe and his pot." There was a gentle rap at the door, and in the easy and familiar manner of the Welsh countryside he shouted to them "Come in whoever you are." In came three fairies disguised as travellers, but Morgan, of course, little suspected that they were other than what they appeared. One of them asked: "Can we beg a little food, good man, to put in this wallet, as we are poor and in want?" Morgan was profuse in his generosity; of course they could: "You are welcome, for as long as my name is Morgan, I will never refuse to those in want." Kindness begets kindness and as the "travellers" were putting some of his proffered bread and cheese in their wallet, they "informed him that as they had it in their power, they would grant him any wish he liked." Now Morgan, who was fond of music, had no difficulty in making up his mind and at once asked for "a harp to play a tune on." Apparently it was more than a fairy gift, it was a fairy harp, which played a lively tune however ill he struck it. No sooner was the request made than the harp was there before him. Very soon his wife came in bringing some friends with her, and Morgan anxious to show his new gift and his skill upon it began to play. So infectious and exhilarating were the melodious strains that poured forth from the fairy harp that the whole company immediately jumped to their feet and began to dance round the room, knocking the chairs over, bumping into tables, jolting one another about and jumping so high some of them that their heads touched the ceiling. Before very long they realised that there was something uncanny in the harp and shouted to Morgan to stop, but Morgan was enjoying himself, heeding not in the least their appeals and imprecations. At last exhausted with his efforts and with laughing at the wild capers he had induced in his friends, he put the harp down. In the end Morgan had a bad name, for his playing "did a considerable damage to the good folks of the neighbourhood, many of whom had their limbs dislocated; for whoever heard the sounds of it could not refrain from dancing." After a very vigorous performance one night "to the great mischief of his neighbours, he was surprised in the morning at not being able to discover the harp anywhere. It was supposed that the fairies . . . feeling compassion for the poor sufferers, deprived Morgan from ever displaying his powers of harmony again."

It would seem that they were almost completely devoid of a sense of humour, though something approaching it, but rather crude and raw, is revealed in one or two of the stories: A native of Nefyn returning from a fair at Pwllheli, saw by *Efail Newydd* a magnificent inn. And though he knew there should be no inn on that spot, still he went towards it and asked one of the servants whether he could stable his horse there. Yes, he could, and the horse was duly put in the stable and he himself went to enjoy a pint of beer—and never in his life had he tasted better beer. Before long he decided he would like to stay the night there and asked if he could have a bed. Yes, he could have a bed, too, and he was led to one gorgeous enough for a king! But, oh! when he

25

awoke in the morning he found himself sleeping on a heap of ashes and his horse tied to a post in the hedge!

Another trick was to tie down a sleeping mortal with gossamer ropes: A farmer's son returning from Beddgelert fair, seeing some fairies dancing and capering, sat down to watch them, and very soon fell asleep. Whether or not the sight of a sleeping mortal was too much of a temptation to them to indulge in a little mischief, they at any rate proceeded to tie him down and that so firmly "that he could not have stirred; then they covered him with a gossamer sheet, so that nobody could see him." Search was made by his family for him but in vain. After a day and a night like that he was released and for some time wandered about not knowing where he was. At cock-crow, however, he came to himself and discovered that he was only a quarter of a mile from home. These were said to be the "mischievous and wanton kind of fairies who dwelt in marshy and rushy places, or among the fern and the heather."

But the grimmest trick of all was played on an old woman who lived at a place called *Hafod Rugog* "in a wild hollow among the mountains." There were many fairies in that neighbourhood and they often came to the old lady to borrow one thing and another. Whether she was getting tired of lending all the time we don't know; she, however, told them one day when they came to borrow again that they could have it if they granted her, first, two wishes—"that the first thing I touch at the door break, and that the first thing I put my hand on in the house be lengthened half a yard." There was a grip stone (*carreg afael*) as it is called, in the wall near the door, which was in her way, and she had in the house a piece of flannel for a jerkin which was half a yard too short. She was out apparently when she met the fairies and made her request, for in coming in, as she was nearing the door "with her kreel full of turf on her back," she unfortunately slipped and, in trying to save herself, put her hand to her knee, which immediately broke. On gaining the house, and forgetting in her pain her second wish, she put her hand to her nose, and lo! it became half a yard longer!

Since I have more than once referred to the story given by

Giraldus Cambrensis it ought now to be given, so that the reader may be made acquainted with the oldest written fairy story we possess.

It will be found in his *Itinerarium Kambriae*, which is a record of a journey that he made through Wales in 1188, in the company of Baldwin, Archbishop of Canterbury, to preach the crusades and to enrol volunteers. It is rather significant that he tells this story when he arrived in the neighbourhood of Neath Valley, for the Vale of Neath has always been noted for its wealth of fairy stories. Indeed it may be that it was along the Neath river that Elidorus found the subterranean passage that led to fairy-land. The last court of the kings and princes of fairydom is said to have been held at *Pen Dinas* in this valley. I should not be a bit surprised to be told that there is still alive a person who has seen them dancing and capering over the precipitous rocks that overlook this river.

Pen Dinas would be an ideal spot in which to hold a court: "That delicate velvet turf on the table-land at the summit of that magnificent, isolated rock must have been a very paradise."

But let Giraldus speak: "A short time before our days, a circumstance worthy of note occurred in these parts, which Elidorus, a priest, most strenuously affirmed had befallen himself. When a youth of twelve years, and learning his letters . . . in order to avoid the discipline and frequent stripes inflicted on him by his preceptor, he ran away, and concealed himself under the hollow bank of a river. After fasting in that situation for two days, two little men of pigmy stature appeared to him, saying, 'If you will come with us, we will lead you to a country full of delights and sports.' Assenting . . . he followed his guides through a path, at first subterranean and dark, into a most beautiful country, adorned with rivers and meadows, woods and plains, but obscure, and not illuminated with the full light of the sun. All the days were cloudy, and the nights extremely dark, on account of the absence of the moon and stars. The boy was brought before the King, and introduced to him in the presence of the court; who, having examined him for a long time, delivered him to his son, who was then a boy. These men were of the smallest stature, but very well proportioned in their make; they were all of a fair complexion, with luxuriant hair falling over their shoulders like that of women. They had horses and greyhounds adapted to their size. They neither ate flesh nor fish, but lived on milk diet, made up into messes with saffron. They never took an oath, for they detested nothing so much as lies. As often as they returned from our upper hemisphere, they reprobated our ambition, infidelities and inconsistencies.

The boy frequently returned to our hemisphere, sometimes by the way he had first gone, sometimes by another . . . and made himself known only to his mother, declaring to her the manners, nature and state of that people. Being desired by her to bring a present of gold, with which that region abounded, he stole, while at play with the king's son, the golden ball with which he used to divert himself, and brought it to his mother in great haste; and when he reached the door . . . but not unpursued . . . his foot stumbled on the threshold, and falling down into the room . . . the two pigmies seized the ball . . . and departed, showing the boy every mark of contempt."

For a long time he tried to discover that subterranean passage again but he never succeeded. He returned to his school and eventually became a priest. "Whenever David II, Bishop of St. David's, talked to him in his advanced state of life concerning this event, he could never relate the particulars without shedding tears."

I mentioned earlier their King—we also know his name— *Gwyn ab Nudd*, a noted figure in Welsh mythology. A very curious story is told of his encounter with the Welsh hermit, St. Collen: Collen one day heard two men talking near the door of his cell about *Gwyn ab Nudd*, and at once told them to go away and not to talk about devils. *Gwyn ab Nudd* got to hear about this and sent for Collen to come to him, but Collen refused; however, in the end he went, taking the precaution to arm himself with a bottle of holy water. When he arrived at the meeting place, the top of a hill, "he saw [there] the fairest castle he had ever beheld, and around it the best appointed troops, and numbers of minstrels, and every kind of music of voice and string, and

steeds with youths upon them . . . and maidens of elegant aspect
. . . and every magnificence becoming the court of a puissant
sovereign. And he beheld a courteous man . . . who bade him
enter, saying the King was waiting for him to come to meat.
And Collen went into the castle, and when he came there the
King was sitting in a golden chair. And he welcomed Collen
honourably and desired him to eat, assuring him that, besides
what he saw he should have the most luxurious of every dainty
and delicacy that the mind could desire . . . 'I will not eat the
leaves of the trees,' said Collen.

'Didst thou ever see men of better equipment than these in red
and blue?' asked the King.

'Their equipment is good enough,' said Collen, 'for such
equipment as it is.'

'What kind of equipment is that?' said the King.

Then said Collen, 'The red on the one part signifies burning,
and the blue on the other signifies coldness.' And with that he
drew out his flask, and threw the holy water on their heads,
whereupon they vanished from his sight, so that there was neither
castle, nor troops, nor men, nor maidens, nor music, nor song,
nor steeds, nor youths, nor banquet, nor the appearance of any
thing whatever, but the green hillocks."

In this chapter, the reader has not forgotten, I hope, that we
were here inquiring into the general character of this fairy tribe—
the *Tylwyth Teg*—as it existed in the peasant mind and as it is
revealed in their stories. It has enabled me, too, to give many
stories which would not fit into any other heading without
making many sub-divisions—and to tell them "in my own way."

Chapter Two

INTO THE ENCHANTED
CIRCLES

OUR largest class of fairy stories is that which relates to the fairy circles and to the fate of the persons who un-wittingly stepped into them. Hardly ever were they released under a year and a day and once in the ring they lost all count of time and might be kept there dancing for five, fifty, even a hundred years and more. With release, dormant mind began to function again, and reawakened memory brought back the task they were engaged in when they stumbled on the enchanted circle. Many, unconscious of the lapse of time, returned to their homes to find strangers there to whom they were utterly unknown, for all memory of them had perished. Few were the districts which could not produce one story of a young man or woman who had been taken away by the fairies.

The first that I shall give comes from north Pembrokeshire and concerns the son and heir of *Llech-y-Deri* farm. He and the head servant, as often happened in the Welsh rural community where class consciousness had never penetrated, were bosom and inseparable friends. In this kindly home they were treated like brothers and if the good mother bought a suit of clothes for her son she bought a similar one at the same time for the servant. In time the two got married to two young women of the neighbourhood, the servant settling down in a cottage on the farm where he continued to work. About six months after the son's marriage the two went out for a day's shooting, and while the servant turned aside to try a rough, difficult but promising corner, something happened to his friend, for on emerging from this corner he could nowhere be found. He looked and searched, whistled and shouted, but to no effect. After a time he decided to return to the farm. No, they had not seen anything of him, and great indeed became their anxiety as he did not return the following night or the following day. Search was made on the spot where the two separated, which revealed nothing, but close by, to their surprise and sorrow, they saw a fairy ring and this brought back to the servant's recollection the fact that he had heard here about the time they parted the sound of sweet and alluring music. They all came to the conclusion that he had stepped into this ring while the fairies were dancing there and had been carried away by them. Weeks and months passed; a child was born to him, years passed and the child grew up. He got married, but to a girl whose family did not enjoy a good reputation for kindness and sympathy. Years passed again, the old folk died, then their daughter-in-law died and *Llech-y-Deri* knew only the grandson and his family.

Sometime after this on a windy, boisterous day in October, a tall, thin, old man, with white beard, whom they took to be some old Jew, was seen coming towards the farmhouse. The mistress, true to her character, laughed at the old man who presented so pathetic a spectacle and lifted the children up to the window to have a look at him. He came up to the door and to their great surprise calmly walked in, and asked for his parents, only to be contemptuously asked in turn what reason he had, "a drunken old Jew," to walk into their house. The old man looked round the house in a lost and surprised manner, being especially baffled it would seem at the sight of the children. He told them it was only the day before he went out shooting and was now returning. The young mistress, however, acquainted him at once with the cruel truth which was to the effect that she had heard that her husband's father had been lost for years, that one day he went out shooting and was never seen again. Her own father, she said, always maintained that he had been murdered: and she became angry again, for the old man made no sign of going. But this roused him, and he declared that the house was his and that he would have his rights. He, however, went out and presently walked over to visit his friend at the cottage, where more surprises still were in store for him. The old man by the fire, as he scrutinised him, began to suspect who he was, and told him of the fateful day fifty years previously when they both went out together for a day's sport. The talk then became general and they exchanged many reminiscences about the days of their youth. As the master of *Llech-y-Deri* was away from home that day the old servant prevailed upon his visitor to stay and have something to eat, but to his horror as he began to eat he fell down dead on the spot.

More usually the stories conclude with the returned person, on being touched or partaking of food, crumbling into a handful of black dust; sometimes even on coming out of the enchanted circle. In this case it was apparently not so, and the lost man was buried by the side of his ancestors, while on *Llech-y-Deri*, because of the rudeness of the young mistress, a curse fell which clung to it for many generations—until the place was sold nine times.

For a much adorned version of this story, with homiletic padding, see *Cymru Fu*, p. 85, under the title *Idwal O Nant Clwyd*.

It wasn't always by accident that people found themselves in these enchanted rings. Quite often the very sight of these care-free folk dancing so merrily proved irresistible: if that failed, the sweet melodious strains of the music supplied the extra attraction needed to pull them in. Two farm servants, Rhys and Llywellyn, were returning from work one evening at dusk when Rhys said he could hear music; his friend, probably preoccupied with the thought of getting home and getting down to his supper, replied that he could hear nothing. Rhys, however, persisted that he had heard music, "a tune to which he danced a hundred times and would again." "You go on," he said, "and I'll catch you up again," and away he bounded, leaving Llywellyn to go home on his own. He was not above suspecting his friend of saying it just to have an excuse to go "off on a spree, and that he would come home drunk before morning." But when morning came and no trace of Rhys, he changed his mind. Search was made for him, but all in vain; days passed, months passed; suspicion began at last to fall on Llywellyn that he had murdered him, and he was put in prison to await his trial. Friends bestirred themselves on his behalf and "a farmer, learned in fairy lore, suspecting how it was, proposed that he and a company of neighbours should go with poor Llywellyn to the spot where he had last seen Rhys."

This was generally done a year and a day after the person's disappearance, and it was of the utmost importance that it should not be delayed beyond that time because the fairies were believed to stay in one place that period of time and then to move off. If he was not rescued then, he might be kept with them for seven, ten or fifty years!

When they arrived at the spot Llywellyn cried, "Hush, I hear music. I hear sweet music of the harps," but the others could hear nothing. Llywellyn put his foot gingerly on the outward edge of the ring and called on one of his friends, David, to put his own foot on his, which he did and immediately heard the music. In turn each of them put his foot on Llywellyn's and in their turn not only heard music but saw great numbers of little people dancing round and round, and Rhys amongst them "dancing like a madman." Llywellyn stood there and watched his chance and as Rhys came whirling by he seized him and pulled him out. Rhys's first question was: "Where are the horses? Where are the horses?" a question which would indicate that on their way home that night they had either been looking for horses or had been working the horses. However, Llywellyn does not seem to have considered it worth a sensible reply, but when Rhys demanded to go back for more music and dancing he thought it was time to give him the brutal truth. "You've been there long enough—long enough to come near getting me hanged, anyhow." They got him home, but Rhys was never the same again, and is said to have died soon afterwards.

Readers will notice that here—as in the story told of the farmer who put his front door at the back to suit a fairy family underneath—putting a foot on that of a fairy, or on that of another person who had the power to see them, conveyed, on the principle of an electric current, the same power to all who did so.

The other story of this class that I am going to give comes from my own home neighbourhood. John, a shoemaker, living near Pencader, had a son named David, who on crossing the *Rhôs* one day inadvertently stepped into a fairy circle, and having danced with them for what seemed to him a few minutes only, found himself outside once more. Either he was released or, in the sweeping movement of a particularly lively dance, he was swung beyond the edge. When he looked round he was astonished to see the whole scene changed. There were roads and houses which he did not remember having seen before, and as he neared home a stranger sight still met his gaze. Instead of the lowly cottage in which he was brought up there now stood a well-built stone farmhouse, with signs of recent cultivation of what in his day was barren upland; strange fields and hedges bewildered him, and a huge dog which he knew was not his old friend *Tango* leaped out and barked savagely at him. He knew, of course, that he had been in a fairy ring, but only for a minute or two, and he put it all down to some illusory or magic creation of the fairies. Was it an imaginary hedge? "He felt, and felt it again—rubbed his eyes, thinking he was dreaming, but a thorn running into his hand convinced him" that it was not so. Confused and bewildered he began to doubt his senses; then he thought he must have lost his way and stopped to take his bearings. But sure enough there was the old *Garreg Hir* on the skyline—an ancient landmark and guide which has immemorially stood here at the junction of three parishes, on a tree-less moorland and close to what must have been until recently a fence-less track.

If fairies loved to roam unmolested over the open heath, heather-
and bracken-grown, they could not find a better paradise than this.
In reference to this ancient stone he again checked up on the
scene, and was confirmed in his first impression that he was of
course near his own home. Presently the farmer came out to see
what the dog was barking at, and when he saw the poor wretch
asked him: "Poor man, who are you?" "I know who I *was*. I
do not know who I am *now*," he replied. "This morning I was
the son of the man who lived in this place"—imagining himself
to be still at the age he was when he went up the *Rhôs*.

The farmer, now suspecting that the poor man had lost his
senses, went on, nevertheless, to explain to him that that farmhouse had been built by his great-grandfather, repaired by his
own grandfather, and greatly added to by himself three years
previously. Still the *Garreg Hir* remained and the rock nearby
where an hour earlier he had robbed a hawk's nest.

Asked where he had been since, he began to tell his story,
which as it came in bits convinced the farmer that he had been
away in the land of the fairies. Upon further questioning he gave
his father's name as John Evan, the shoemaker, of *Glanrhyd*, and
as the farmer had never heard of either—the farm having been
given another name—he decided, after he had given him something to eat, to take him over to *Cati Shîn* (an old-fashioned
form of the modern name Catherine Jones), for *Cati* was old and
full of ancient lore. Having finished their meal they started on
their way to *Cati*. As they were walking, the stranger gradually
fell behind; the farmer however did not think much of that,
possibly imagining that the "old man" was feeling his years, but
when he heard the footsteps getting fainter and fainter, he turned
round and was only just in time to see him falling and disinte-
grating into "about a thimbleful of black ashes."

Much upset by such a sight he, nevertheless, decided to go
forward. When he unfolded his strange story to *Cati* she told him
that she had a faint recollection of having heard from her grandfather, *Evan Shenkin*, of *Penferdir*, of John Evan the shoemaker,
and that he had a son who was lost on the moors and was never
heard of again. It was believed that the fairies had taken him. His

father's cottage did stand, she said, near the farmhouse—so the "boy" was quite right after all.

Many fairies used to be seen on these uplands and, as I said, if they wanted a fairy paradise, here it was. A woman is said to have caught one once, who lived with her for many years, but one day the call of the magic circle and the dance came and she never saw him again. And yet it was believed in parts of Cardiganshire that once a fairy attached himself to one he could not be easily got rid of, for they "were little beings of a very devoted nature."

One could give many examples of such stories from every part of Wales. They have many features in common: two men going out together, one is suddenly and mysteriously lost. The other returns home, is suspected of murdering him, is imprisoned, friends consult the wise man who usually advises going to the exact spot in a year and a day, and sometimes recommends that the companion be dressed in exactly the same manner as on the day he lost his friend. On being recovered from the magic ring the "lost" person's first question was about the task he was engaged in when he disappeared. None were said to recover fully from their experience and their life was short; but if they had been away many years, on partaking of food or on being touched they crumbled into a few specks of black dust.

There were various means of getting them out of the enchanted rings, but the greatest care had to be exercised that in the attempt no one put his foot inside the ring. One method was to take a rowan stick, stand on the edge of the circle and extend it as far into it as possible—the fairies hated the rowan tree as much as they hated iron. A story comes from Cardiganshire of a girl who was got out in this way. She was invisible to her rescuers but she could see them and the rowan stick, which, as she came round in the dance, she grasped and the spell was broken.

Another way often adopted was one in which the rescuer stood on the edge of the circle and watched his chance as the person came whizzing by in the dance to grasp him by the arm or flowing garment.

To take a piece of iron and "dexterously" touch a person with it "and snatch him out" was another method.

Sometimes the rescuer took great risks and went right into the circle, but only after taking the greatest precautions as was done in a case related from Anglesey: A man named Evan Griffith and his daughter had been all day searching for a lost cow, and coming home in the evening they saw a lot of fairies on their ponies galloping about in a ring. "The daughter, in her eagerness to behold the little knights more closely, got unawares within the circle." The poor father had now two things to look for, but he forgot the first in his anxiety for his daughter. After a few days he decided to consult a wise man, who told him he would have her back on the anniversary of her disappearance. But he was to take four stalwart men with him, tie a rope round his waist and in this manner to venture into the very circle itself. When the day came they were all there, and the father "beheld his daughter riding round in great state. In he rushed and snatched her, and thanks to his friends (who pulled him out by means of the rope) he got her out of the fairy ring before the little men had time to think of it."

Carrying a knife was supposed to be a sufficient precaution. In the case of the lake fairies of "*Llyn Urddyn* between the western slopes of the Llawllech in Merionethshire" a person was safe if he walked on the grass and kept away from the shore "and the stony places," for otherwise they might suddenly pick him up and carry him through the air, but if he took hold of a blade of grass, they had not the power to break it, indeed dared not injure one single blade.

This last story, like that of the shoemaker's son, comes from my home district of Pencader, and has stronger affinities with the *Mabinogion* than with the usual fairy story, for the long absence is attributed not to stepping into a fairy ring but to the enchantment caused by the singing of a bird. Readers of the *Mabinogion* will remember how the birds of Rhiannon had such power to charm that years passed away as a single day. Briefly the story is this: *Bendigeid Vran's* sister, *Branwen*, was married to an Irish king, who seems not to have possessed the energy or the power to protect her from the insults and the ill-treatment of his foster-brothers. To get a message over to her brother at Harlech was impossible, so she "reared a starling in the cover of the kneading trough, and taught it to speak, and she taught the bird what manner of man her brother was. And she wrote a letter of her woes, and the despite with which she was treated, and she bound the letter to the root of the bird's wing, and sent it towards Britain. And the bird came to the Island, and one day it found *Bendigeid Vran* at *Caer Seiont* in *Arvon* . . . and it alighted on his shoulder and ruffled its feathers, so that the letter was seen, and they knew that the bird had been reared in a domestic manner. Then *Bendigeid Vran* took the letter . . . and when he had read (it) he grieved exceedingly." At once he decided to gather together a mighty host and invade Ireland, "but they were not victorious, for only seven men of them all escaped, and *Bendigeid Vran* himself was wounded in the foot with a poisoned dart." Before he died he asked the seven to cut off his head and take it with them to London and bury it on the White Mount with the face towards France. So they started on their journey and came to Harlech, Bran's home, where "they sat down to eat and to drink and there came three birds, and began singing unto them a certain song, and all the songs they had ever heard were unpleasant compared thereto; and the birds seemed to them to be at a great distance from them over the sea, yet they appeared as distinct as if they were close by, and at this repast they continued seven years."

And now to return to *Pant Shôn Shenkin*: One fine summer morning young Shôn was on his way out to the fields when he heard a little bird singing in a nearby tree—so sweet and enchanting was it that he sat down under the tree to listen to it, yes, to listen until that song should cease. In a few minutes he got up again, but was astonished to see that the young tree under which he sat had not only grown into a huge tree, but was now in an advanced stage of decay. He made for his home where he had further surprises: that too had changed and was in the possession of an old man he had never seen before. Shôn very naturally asked him what he was doing there, whereupon the old man became rather testy and asked him what right had he to insult him in his own home. The lad then asked what had become of

Shôn Sat under the Tree to Listen

his father and mother who were there when he left earlier in the morning. He related the story of the little bird and the withered tree which brought back to the old man what he had often heard his grandfather say, how that his father's brother had gone out one morning and was never seen again. "Is your name John?" he asked. "Come and embrace your nephew. Old *Cati Madlein* of Brechfa said that you were under the power of the fairies, and would not be released until the last sap of the sycamore tree would be dried up". And so they embraced, but in that embrace poor Shôn crumbled into dust.

Longfellow's story of the "Golden Legend" will at once suggest itself to the reader, in which we are told that the monk Felix spent a hundred years, held spell-bound by the singing of that snow-white bird, and it all passed like one hour.

The monk returned to the monastery to find a new Prior there and new faces everywhere, though the place itself was still the same. Felix was puzzled for only that morning had he gone out for a little walk, but no one knew him. An aged monk, however, remembered that in his early novitiate a monk had gone away and never returned. Books were brought out, dates were consulted, yes, it was quite true, a hundred years previously a monk had walked out and never come back.

> And they knew at last,
> That such had been the power
> Of that celestial and immortal song.
> A hundred years had passed,
> And had not seemed so long
> As a single hour.

Chapter Three

BABY-SNATCHING

WE feel now that we are leaving the world of the happy, honest and kindly small folk who came out with the evening mist and setting sun to while away the moonlit nights in dancing to sweet music, when we come to deal with those who lurked about human habitations and stole whatever of value they could lay hands on—even the babies in their cradles, leaving in their place their own peevish, ugly little brats. The countryside was aware of the existence of more than one kind of fairies, and some of them they dreaded, though Hugh Evans does not seem to have heard about any except the happy, kindly, care-free, dancing folk who were the only ones round his own home, and thinks that fairies have been accused of thefts committed by others. Still there is too much evidence to the contrary, and a whole cycle of stories from every part of Wales testifies to their existence and wicked practices. Let us hear what another North Wales writer has to say: "Fairies were not all of the same species, but were almost all associated with hilly districts. They varied according to the districts to which they belonged. . . . In some districts the fairies were described as diminutive beings with strong thieving propensities; who used to live in summer among the bracken in the mountains and in winter among the heather and gorse. These used to frequent fairs, and steal the farmers' money from their pockets, placing in their stead the coins of the fairies which counterfeited the ordinary money; but when they were paid for anything that had been bought, they would vanish in the seller's pocket.

"In other districts they were described as somewhat bigger and stronger people; but these were also of a thieving disposition and would lurk about people's houses, watching their opportunity to steal the butter and cheese from the dairy. They would also loiter about the cow-yards and would sometimes milk the cows and the goats. . . . But the greatest sport this species had was in stealing unbaptised babies. . . . They are said to dwell in the secret caves of the mountains . . . and that if anyone could come across the mouth of the cave he would find an immense amount of wealth 'for they were uncomparable thieves'."

The species that we have so far been dealing with had their abode in "rushy valleys or *cymoedd*, surrounded by grassy hills and the brinks of rivers and lakes. . . . These are also said to have lived under the earth and the ways leading to their country lay under hollow banks overhanging the deepest parts of the lakes, or the deepest pools of rivers, so that no mortal might follow them farther than the water's edge."

But we must leave these kindly folk and come to those who, on every opportunity they had, stole their neighbours' babies.

Belief in changelings was not confined to Wales; it was common in Scotland, England and Ireland. Thus Spenser, in his *Faerie Queene*:

> And her base elfin brood there for thee left;
> Such, men do changelings call, so changed by Fairies theft.

The first story comes from the neighbourhood of Llanidloes in mid-Wales; indeed variants of it have been found in many parts of the country and even in Brittany: A cottager and his wife had twins whom the mother "nursed with great care and tenderness. Some months afterwards indispensable business called her to the house of one of her nearest neighbours," and though it was not far she yet did not like to leave them on their own in the cradle, because her house was rather isolated; besides she had heard many a time that goblins or fairies haunted the neighbourhood. She was not, however, long away but on the way home she became rather terrified as she saw "some of the old elves in blue petticoats" lurking about. When she got back she found to her great relief that her babies were there and everything as she left it. In time, however, it was discovered that the twins made no progress and the father became apprehensive. Indeed he went so far as to declare that they were not their children at all, but the mother would have it that they were, until there arose quite a squabble between them. At last she decided to go and consult a *gwr cyfarwydd* (i.e. a wise man, or a conjurer) who gave her the following directions, to be followed very carefully: "When you are preparing dinner for the reapers (it was the time of the rye and oat harvest) empty the shell of a hen's egg, and boil the shell full of pottage and take it out through the door as if you meant it for a dinner to the reapers, and then listen what the twins will say." The mother did as she was told and on the way out stopped to listen; to her astonishment she heard one of the twins say to the other:

> "*Gwelais vesen cyn gweled derwen,*
> *Gwelais wy cyn gweled iâr,*
> *Erioed ni welais verwi bwyd i vedel*
> *Mewn plisgyn wy iâr!*"

> "Acorns before oak I knew,
> An egg before a hen,
> Never one hen's egg-shell stew
> Enough for harvest man!"

The mother knew now what to do, which was to carry out the rest of the wise man's directions and throw the changelings into a nearby pool. In an instant the wicked fairies were on the spot to save their kin and at the same time she had her own children back.

The Breton legend runs like this: A mother whose child had been exchanged for one of the fairies "was advised by the Virgin

Mary to prepare a meal for ten farm-servants in an egg-shell. . . ."
This she did and the changeling asked what she was about. She
told him. Whereupon he exclaimed: "A meal for ten, dear
mother, in one egg-shell?" He then recited in his native tongue
the following rhymed triad, the exact version of which M. Ville-
marque found in the county of Glamorgan:

> "Gweliz mez ken gwelet derven,
> Gweliz vi ken gwelet iar wenn.
> Erioez ne wiliz evelhenn.

Welsh readers will have no difficulty at all in understanding this,
but for the sake of English readers here is a translation:

> I have seen the acorn before I saw the oak,
> I have seen the egg before I saw the white hen.
> I have never seen the like of this.

The mother told him that he had seen far too many things and
that he was going to have a good thrashing which she proceeded
to administer. When he began to bawl a "fairy came and took
him away, leaving the stolen child sleeping sweetly in the cradle."

The second, in which the procedure was varied, comes from
Capel Curig in North Wales: A farmer's wife had given birth to
a bonny baby at the beginning of the harvest, but as the weather
was wretched, and the farm a considerable distance from her
place of worship, she neglected to baptise it before the usual
eighth day. In the midst of this unsettled weather there came one
fine day, and she felt she ought to do all she could to save the
harvest. So she went into the field, leaving the baby in the charge
of its grandmother, an aged and feeble person, who very soon
fell asleep. This was the fairies' chance, and they took it. The
changeling soon began to whine and groan and wake up the old
lady. When she went to the cradle "she saw a slender, wizened
old man moving restlessly and peevishly about. 'Alas! Alas!'
said she, 'the Old Tylwyth have been here'; and she at once blew
the horn to call the mother home, who came without delay."
She ran at once to the cradle, lifted the child out, hugged him,
sang a lullaby to him and in every way tried to soothe him, but to

no avail; he still continued to scream. Then she had a look at him and perceived at once to her horror that he was not her child at all, and the more she examined him the uglier he seemed. She sent for her husband and told him to look at once for a *gwr cyfarwydd*, a skilled man. Somebody told him that the parson of Trawsfynydd was skilled in the secrets of the spirits; so he went to him." The parson directed him to take a shovel, cover it with salt and cut the figure of the cross in the salt; then to take it to the room where the changeling was and, after opening the window, to put it on the fire until the salt was burnt. This they did and when the salt got white hot the "peevish abortion" (*erthyl croes*) vanished unseen by anybody, and on the doorstep they found their own child, whole and unscathed. It seems that in Scotland, too, fire was made use of in order to detect a changeling and force him to quit.

From Llanfabon in the county of Glamorgan comes a case where a very long and complicated procedure had to be adopted. This place was noted for its ugly and wicked fairies, who in addition to stealing babies delighted in leading travellers out of their way, luring them by their music into dangerous and desolate bogs.

One of the children they stole was little Griff, a little fellow of 3, the only child of his mother, and she was a widow. Knowing of the existence of these wicked fairies about the place she took especial care of Griff, so much so that the neighbours said she was too anxious about him and that some misfortune would surely befall him one day.

One day she heard a moaning noise coming from the direction of the cow-shed and in case anything had happened to one of the cattle she ran there in great fright, leaving the little fellow in the house and the door wide open. Who can describe the shock she had on returning and finding he was not there! She searched everywhere, but in vain; towards sunset, however, the little chap turned up and said quite plainly, "Mother." She looked at him for some time and in the end said, "You are not my child." "I am, indeed," he replied. After this he remained with her for a whole twelvemonth, but she was not at all happy about things.

"The Changeling Vanished"

Griff was a growing boy but this child made no progress at all and was every day getting uglier. At last she decided to go to a cunning man (*dyn hysbys*) who after listening to her story said: "He is a *Crimbil* right enough and your child is with the old *Bendith* somewhere. But if you will follow carefully my instructions the child will soon be restored to you. About noon tomorrow take an egg and cut it in half, throw one half away but keep the other in your hand and begin to mix its contents. See that the 'little man' is somewhere near and taking notice of what you're doing, but don't call his attention to it, try and engage his interest without actually calling him and very likely he will ask what you are doing. You tell him that you are mixing a pasty for the reapers and let me know what answer he will give."

The mother returned home and the next day followed out to the letter the cunning man's instructions. The little man stood by her side and watched her intently; presently he said: "Mother, what are you doing?" "Mixing a pasty for the reapers, my son." "O, is that it? I heard from my father and he from his father who had heard it from his own father that the acorn was before the oak and that the oak was in the earth, but I never heard of nor have I seen anybody mixing the reapers' pasty in an egg-shell." She noticed that as he said this he looked very cross which added to his ugliness and made him most repulsive to her.

That same afternoon she returned to the cunning man to inform him of what he said. "O," he replied, "he is one of the old *breed* right enough. Now, the next full moon will be in four days and you must go at midnight to where the four roads meet above *Rhyd Y Gloch*. Hide yourself in a spot where you can obtain a full view of the openings to the cross roads, and if you see anything that would rouse you, restrain yourself and remember to remain perfectly still, otherwise the plan will miscarry and you will never get your child back."

These instructions bewildered and mystified her, but she had not long to wait and at the appointed hour she was safely ensconced behind a big bush which still gave her command of the meeting roads. For a long time she watched and listened; at last she heard the strains of distant music approaching. Nearer and nearer it came until at last it was by her side and she realised it was a procession of *Bendith y mamau* (the fairies) on its way somewhere. In the middle of the procession of many hundreds "she saw a sight that pierced her heart and caused her blood to stop in her veins," for there, walking between four fairies, was her own Griff. Her first impulse was to spring out and rescue him, but she remembered the advice of the cunning man and stood still.

After the procession had passed and the music had died away in the distance she came out of her hiding place and directed her steps towards home. Convinced now that the "child" who claimed to be her son was one of the old *breed* she did not know how to contain her hatred and loathing; she was, however, given sufficient strength not to show her feelings. Back again she went the following day to tell the cunning man all she had seen the night before and to ask for further instructions. He seems to have been expecting her, and after hearing what she had to say, he opened a big book over which he pored for a long time. Recovery was evidently going to be a difficult matter. He now informed her that she must get a black hen, without a single white feather, or, indeed, a feather of any other colour, and kill it, then put it, feathers and all, before a log fire to bake it. Immediately she did this "she was to stop every hole and entrance into the building except one and not to take much notice of the *crimbil* until the hen was done and all the feathers had fallen from her, and then to look where he was."

Strange as it all seemed she decided to give it a try, and as she could find no hen amongst her own that met the requirements she went from farm to farm without any success, but as she was just on the point of giving up she managed to get one. After returning home she prepared the fire and put the hen before it, having in the meantime forgotten all about the *crimbil* and fallen into a kind of trance from which she was awakened by the sound of music outside the house—like the music she had heard at the cross roads. The feathers had now fallen away from the hen, and when she came to look round the *crimbil* had vanished. Wildly she looked about the house and to her great joy heard the voice of little Griff outside calling her. She dashed out to him and hugged him, asking where he'd been all that time, but he could give her no account of anything beyond saying that he had been listening to sweet music. She noticed that he was rather thin and looked worn in appearance. And that's the end of the story of the lost child. Hartland gives an example of the use of a black hen from "the north-east of Scotland . . . where a beggar, who had diagnosed a changeling, was allowed to try his hand at disposing of it; he made a large fire on the hearth and held a black hen over it till she struggled, and finally escaped from his grasp, flying out by the 'lum'."

Certain precautions could of course be taken—and were taken: One was to have the children baptised as early as possible for they took no child that had a name. If this had been neglected there could be put up against the cradle the poker or the tongs— or a knife inside it—for a fairy would never come near iron. Constant vigilance was essential on *Nos Wyl Ifan*, St. John's Eve, for this kind of fairy was believed to be particularly busy at that time. In order to discover whether a puny, peevish child was a changeling or not, an ignorant mother would hold it "on a shovel over the fire" or bathe it "in a solution of fox-glove, which kills it." Another practice was to leave it out "all night under an oak tree in the belief that thus cruelly abandoned the fairies would come" for it. The suspected changeling could be neglected generally and given nothing to eat; it could again be thrown into a river or a pond, for if it belonged to them it was believed that the fairies would be soon on the spot to rescue it.

These are cruel practices; they belong not to Wales in particular, but have been noted in Ireland, Denmark and Sweden, for it was a widely held belief—even the great reformer, Luther, was in favour of throwing them into a river.

Only male infants were stolen; there does not seem to be on record a case in which a baby girl was taken.

Despite all the care taken and the many ways adopted of discovering a changeling, some did grow up in human homes, but they could easily be recognised. They were smaller, less proportionate in their build—having long bodies and short legs, often bandy legs. They were irritable and snappy, jealous and suspicious in their nature and often exhibited fits of uncontrollable temper. These must not be confused with the children of mixed marriages who often were extremely handsome and gifted.

It was believed by some that the reason for their exchange of babies was their desire to improve their race and introduce healthy, well-formed children and get rid of some of their puny ill-shaped offspring, but that is hardly a satisfactory explanation. "In Scotland . . . it was once thought that the fairies were obliged every seventh year to pay to the great enemy of mankind an offering of one of their own children, or a human child instead . . . hence the reason for exchanging."

While we are on the subject of protection from the unwelcome attentions of fairies, there was another way of keeping them away from one, and that was to build up around the house—or the bed, as in this case—a hedge of furze. A resident of Anglesey used to visit an old woman of the name of Betty Griffith who lived in a small dark cottage with only one tiny window. On entering she saw a huge "barricade of thick gorse, so closely packed and piled up that no bed was to be seen." Upon being asked if it was on account of the cold that she built up this solid fence she replied that indeed it was not but in order to keep away the fairies who had taken to annoying her, spilling her tea, turning the milk sour, sitting on the table and generally mocking her. Behind this barricade of furze she managed to get peace; "they cannot get through this, it pricks them so bad."

Chapter Four

FAIRY MOTHERS

THERE is a considerable group of stories which reveals the preference of fairy mothers for human midwives. They come from both North and South Wales and have certain features in common: The midwives are usually fetched by the fairy father on horseback, then somewhere before they reach their destination some sort of mist is cast over their eyes so that they can see nobody but the mother and the child and those in attendance. Then accidentally in bathing the baby they put a finger, wet with the fairy soap or ointment used in the operation, to an itching eye, and behold! everything becomes visible to them.

But this is not said to have happened in the case of the midwife from Nant Gwynen in North Wales who had just gone to perform a similar duty at a place called *Hafodydd Brithion*. While there a gentleman rode up to the door on a fine grey horse and bade her accompany him immediately. There was so much authority in his voice that the poor woman had not the courage to say no, much as it was her duty to remain where she was. So she mounted his horse behind him, and away they went, as if on swallow's wings, through *Cwmllan*, over *Bwlch Cwmllan*, down *Nant yr*

Aran and over the *Gadair*, to *Cwm Hafod Ruffydd*, and that before
she had time to say "Boo." When she reached there, she saw a
grand palace right in front of her, most beautifully lit up with
lamps, the like of which she had never seen before. They entered
the court, and a crowd of attendants, clad in the costliest of gar-
ments, came out to meet them. She was immediately led through
a large hall into a bed-chamber, which surpassed in splendour
anything she had ever seen before. She was treated with great
consideration by everybody, and later declared that it was the
most pleasant episode in her life. "She saw nothing but ceaseless
merriment both night and day: dancing, singing, and continual
fun." When she left, having performed her duties with great
satisfaction, she was given by the gentleman a purse, and charged
not to open it until she got home. She was brought home along
the same path as she had gone but by one of the servants this time.
On opening her purse she found it full of money which lasted her
until she died.

In the case of the midwife from Llanuwchllyn, she saw nothing
but the father and mother and the child. In bathing the baby she
was given a special kind of water and told not to get any of it on
her eyes. She complied with the request seeing nothing unreason-
able in it. However, in the course of one of the bathings her eye
happened to itch and she rubbed it with her finger. There must
have been some of the forbidden water on it for apparently after
that she could always see fairies, and happening to be on the street
in Bala one day, whom should she see but the husband of the fairy
she attended. She asked him, naturally, how the little family was;
he looked at her in great surprise and asked her with what eye she
could see him. She answered, the left. With that he touched it, and
immediately became invisible.

Something similar happened to a midwife from *Garth Dorwen*,
but the story starts further back. With her husband she went one
day to All Hallows fair at Caernarvon to hire a servant-maid. It
was the custom then for the young men and women who wished
to be hired to stand at a certain place, to which the old couple
directed their steps. There they saw a very beautiful girl with
golden hair, standing a little apart from the others. The old lady

"Over Hedges, Rocks, Woods and Valleys"

went up to her and asked her if she wanted a place; she replied that she did. She was immediately hired and went to her place at the appointed time. In those days it was the custom, after supper, during the long winter nights for the womenfolk to do the spinning, but the maid used to go to do hers out in the meadow by the light of the moon. There the *Tylwyth Teg* were in the habit of coming to her to sing and dance. But sometime in the Spring, Eilian (for such was her name) went away with the fairies and she was never seen again. Now the old lady of *Garth Dorwen* used to act as midwife and was in great demand for that purpose.

One moonlit night, with a light drizzle and a thin fog hanging about, behold a gentleman comes to the door to fetch her to his wife. She got up behind him and they rode as far as *Rhos y Cowrt*. Here they entered a large cave and then on to a chamber where the wife lay in bed. It was the most beautiful place the old lady had ever seen in her life. She performed her duties successfully and went to the fire to dress the baby. After she had finished, the husband brought her a bottle of ointment to anoint the baby's eyes, warning her at the same time not to let any of it touch her own eyes. But somehow, after putting the bottle away, one of her eyes began to itch and she rubbed it with that finger with which she had anointed the baby's eyes, and lo and behold! the whole scene was changed. With that eye she saw that the poor wife was lying on a bundle of rushes and withered bracken in a large cave with big stones all around her, and a miserable little fire in one corner. She saw, too, that it was Eilian, her old servant maid. With the other eye the place still appeared the finest she had ever seen.

Some time afterwards she went to Caernarvon market and happening to see the strange gentleman asked him how Eilian was. "Oh she's very well. With what eye do you see me?" "With this," she replied, pointing to it. He took a bulrush and in an instant pulled her eye out.

Instances are also found in the folk-lore of other nations where fairies are said to help girls to spin straw and gold, but always on some condition which it is afterwards found difficult to fulfil.

It may have been that in Eilian's case that help was dependent upon a promise of marriage.

The next story comes from the banks of the Teifi, and concerns one Pali, who was once called upon to attend the wife of one of the fairy princes. How she got to fairy-land we are not told, probably on horseback as in the case of most of the others, riding pillion behind the prince and flying over hedges, rocks, woods and valleys. However, when she got there she was ushered into a very grand palace where everything had been arranged in the most exquisite fashion: the mother was dressed in white and lay on a white bed, indeed everything in the room was set out in white. Pali, who had sole charge of mother and baby, fared very sumptuously, but who attended on the three of them she had no idea, for everything was done secretly and noiselessly. She got on excellently with the mother who was a person of charming disposition and temperament, but anybody else she never saw and would be quite ignorant of their existence except for the prompt and excellent attendance. She was given a particular ointment to use on the baby and charged not to let any of it get into her eyes; but one day while she was dressing him her eye began to itch and she rubbed it with her hand. Then the whole scene changed and amongst the many wonders that had before baffled her, that of the silent but efficient service was revealed as being carried out by small men and small women who "following a variety of occupations were in their movements . . . as light as the morning breeze." To move about was no trouble to them at all, and they brought things into the room with the liveliest speed. They prepared dainty food for the confined lady with the utmost order and skill, and the air of kindliness and affection with which they waited on her was truly remarkable. In the evening when she had finished her duties and just in order to keep the conversation going she said idly, "You have had a great many visitors today." But its effect on the mother and her reply surprised her very much. "How do you know that? Have you been putting the ointment on your eyes?" and with that she jumped out of bed and blew into her face, saying, "Now you will see no more." After that she was never able to see fairies.

There is a variant ending which says that Pali was entrusted with the ointment again on promising not to rub it into her eyes, but it was widely believed that she broke her promise and was able to see fairies all her life.

According to another variant, which comes from the northern part of the same county, the end was not yet: Pali one day went to *Ffair Rhos* and saw a large number of fairies there, amongst them the princess whom she had attended. Urged by the happy recollection of the good time she had when attending to her she went up to her—but again did the wrong thing and said the wrong thing, for the lady flew into a rage and "asked her how she could see her, and spat in her face, which put . . . an end for ever to her power of seeing her or anybody of her race." Readers will note the similarity here to the incidents on the streets of Bala and Caernarvon.

Chapter Five

FAIRY VENGEANCE

THE first story tells of the dreadful vengeance wreaked by the fairies upon the remote descendants of one unfriendly farmer and comes from the pen of Mr. Craigfryn Hughes, the author of the novel *Y Ferch O Gefn Ydfa* (The Maid of Cefn Ydfa), a Glamorgan man whose grandmother—from whom he heard it—was born in 1773 near Pontypool. She remembered well the Reverend Edmund Jones, folklorally speaking, of blessed memory.

"In one of the centuries gone by, there lived a husbandman on the farm of *Pantannas* (in the eastern corner of the parish of Merthyr Tydfil), and at that time the fairies used to pay frequent visits to several of his fields," but he entertained no friendly feelings towards the "noisy, boisterous and pernicious tribe." Indeed he very much wanted to get rid of them, and in the pursuit of his purpose went to consult an old witch who agreed to help him on condition that she had the whole of one evening's milk. She advised him to plough up all their circles and favourite resorts. This he did and the fairies left. He sowed various seed in a field where they were fond of congregating and it looked healthy and promising. But one evening when he was returning home "he was met by a diminutive being in the shape of a little man with a red coat on. When he had come right up to him, he unsheathed his little sword, and, directing the point towards the farmer, he said:

"*Dial a ddaw*   "Vengeance cometh
Y mae gerllaw."   Fast it approacheth."

The farmer tried to laugh it off, but there was something in the stern looks of the little man that made him feel uncomfortable. A few nights later when going to bed the family was terribly frightened by "a noise as though the house were falling to pieces" followed by the warning words:

"*Daw dial.*"   "Vengeance cometh."

At harvest time when they were about to haul the heavy yield of that promising field, behold! one night the whole crop was burnt up and the barn as well. "The day after . . . as he was surveying the destruction . . . behold! the little fellow, who had met him a few days before, met him again, and with a challenging glance, he pointed his sword towards him saying:

"*Nid yw ond dechreu!*"   "It but beginneth!"

The farmer now became really frightened and called the little man back to tell him that if they called their vengeance off he would allow the grass to grow again in their favourite spots and rings. "No," was his angry reply, "the word of the king has been given, and he will avenge himself on thee to the utmost of his power; and there is no power on the face of creation that will cause it to be withdrawn."

Overcome by the thought of the continued hostility of the fairies the farmer broke down—he had already had his barn and his field of oats destroyed—"and it but beginneth!" The little man was adamant, but seeing the tears of the farmer he said he would see his master about it and meet him there again on the third day at the hour of sunset. When the farmer arrived on the third day, the little man was already there: The king had given his consideration to the matter, but his decrees were immutable;

however, in view of the farmer's changed attitude the threatened vengeance would be delayed beyond his own days and those of his children. This greatly calmed the mind of the farmer and he must have been glad to see them back once more in their favourite spots. "A century passed" and though the warning voice was heard at intervals the fact that nothing happened bred in the family a false sense of security. They went about their duties in the normal way, were married and given in marriage: Rhydderch the heir of *Pontannas* became betrothed to Gwerfyl the daughter of a neighbouring farm, *Pen Craig Daf*, and the wedding day was fixed. At the intervening Christmas the young woman came to spend the day at *Pontannas*, and after feasting off roast goose they sat round the fire to listen to the tales of their seniors when suddenly, from the bed of the river, there arose a piercing shriek: "*Daeth amser ymddial!*" "The time for revenge has come!"

They went out and listened; it came again. They were greatly disturbed, but what did it mean? Apparently this generation knew nothing of the original offence of their ancestor or of the vengeance that threatened them. They returned to the house where another frightful experience was to befall them, for the whole building shook "to its very foundations." This was not all. "A little woman made her appearance on the table . . . near the window. 'What dost thou, ugly little thing, want here?' asked one of those present.

"'I have nothing to do with thee, O man of the meddling tongue,' said the little woman, 'but I have been sent here to recount some things which are about to happen to this family and another family in the neighbourhood, things that might be of interest to them, but as I have received such an insult from the black fellow that sits in the corner, the veil that hides them from their sight shall not be lifted by me'."

She refused any further information but darkly hinted that "a certain maiden's heart is like a ship on the coast, unable to reach the harbour because the pilot has lost heart," and she vanished, no one knew whither or how. Once more the shrieks from the river were renewed and were kept up for a long time—"The time of vengeance has come."

In spite of their fear and dread, the time of parting had come and Gwerfyl had to return home. Rhydderch went with her, but was never seen again. It was thought that he was lured into one of the fairy rings and carried to a cave in *Darren y Cigfrain* (The Ravens' Rift).

Back at the homes of the young people a new anxiety ruled. Worried and anxious they decided to consult an aged hermit, *Gweirydd*, who lived in an underground cave and was regarded as a *dewin* (a sorcerer). He was unable to offer them any comfort, rather the reverse. When they told him of the little woman and the piercing shriek from the river the night Rhydderch was lost "he informed them that it was the judgment threatened to the family by the fairies that had overtaken the youth, and that it was useless for them to think of ever seeing him again." He might return in future generations, but not in their time.

"Time rolled on . . . years passed away like smoke, and generations like the shadows of the morning, and there was no longer anyone alive who remembered Rhydderch." While she lived his betrothed daily ascended a small hill to watch and wait. Her eyesight began to fail and yet she gazed, "till full of days . . . death put an end to all her hopes," and she was buried at the *Fan* Chapel.

Back in the cave, after staying there as he thought only a few days, Rhydderch asked permission to go home, which the king readily granted. It was a fine summer afternoon and he went towards the *Fan* but was surprised to see no chapel there, then to *Pen Craig Daf* to see his beloved. As nobody had heard of Gwerfyl they "took him for a madman." It was the same at *Pontannas*: nobody knew him, though the farmer had, long ago, heard something from his grandfather that "some hundreds of years previously" a youth had suddenly disappeared.

Accidentally his stick touched Rhydderch and he "vanished in a shower of dust. Nothing more was ever heard of him." Still some voice, now that it was all over, could proclaim, if not from the bottom of the river-bed, from some other quarter:

"*Mae'r dial drosodd.*"   "Vengeance is over."

Of a different character still is this next vengeance-story, and I was much surprised to find it included in a collection of fairy stories, but it has points of interest—the story of the *Gwylliaid Cochion Mawddwy*. To me *Gwylliaid* always meant bandits or robbers, and that is what the red-haired band of Mawddwy were. *Gwyllion* (see Anwyl's Dictionary) include: witch, hag, ghost or goblin, and Wirt Sikes speaks of *Gwyllion* as "female fairies . . . who haunt lonely roads in the Welsh mountains and lead night-wanderers astray." Owen is evidently inclined to accept this interpretation and in support refers to the *Llanfrothen Legend*. It is the story of a young man's marriage with a lake maiden, where one meets the usual warning about touching with iron. It however accidentally happened, but her husband pleaded with her to stay with him, if only for the sake of the children: "What will become of our children without their mother?" She seemed, as in the majority of cases in this group, to be utterly indifferent: "*Gadewch iddynt fod yn bennau cochion a thrwynau hirion!*"—"Let them be red-headed and long-nosed!"

"That a race of men having these characteristics did exist in Wales is undoubted . . . a strong tribe . . . tall and athletic, and lived by plunder." The reader will pardon me for giving so much time to the red-haired tribe, but they have long interested me because I belong to a pocket of red-haired people who have long inhabited the lordship of Emlyn on the banks of the Teifi. The description "tall and athletic" suits them admirably, but they have not the long nose.

The red bandits of Mawddwy lived by open plunder, driving sheep and cattle away to their dens and generally terrorising the countryside. Such a menace did they become that two local magnates, John Wynn of *Gwydir* and Baron Owen, raised a body of stout men to track them to their lair and destroy them. Amongst those captured was the youngest son of an aged mother who pleaded tearfully for the life of this one to be spared, but without avail. When the pitiless sheriff declared that he, too, must hang like the others, she bared her withered and yellowed breasts before him and said:"These have given suck to those who will one day wash their hands in thy life's blood!" And it was so!

She knew her brood only too well. This must have been the most dramatic incident in any court of law in Wales, and must have sent a shudder of disgust and horror through the whole court truly prophetic of the revenge she foretold.

As the sheriff was one day returning past the scene of the slaughter, a tree fell across the road in front of him, and the brigands rushed out and murdered him. It is said that they had fled some distance when they remembered their mother's words, and feeling it an obligation on them to carry them out literally, returned and "thrust their swords into the baron's breast and washed their hands in his heart's blood."

These were disturbed times following upon the Wars of the Roses and the wars of independence of Owen Glyndwr; indeed, it may have been an endemic state of disorder, where the native population, oppressed, and ousted from their settlements, took to the woods and mountains and lived by plunder. Sir John Wynn of *Gwydir* tells how his great-grandfather durst not go to church on Sundays without leaving behind a band of men to guard the house, and another man on a vantage point, placed so as to command a view of both church and house, to raise a hue and cry if the house was attacked.

It reads to me more like a chapter out of a history book than out of a fairy book, though they may have been held to have fairy blood in their veins. And yet Sir John Rhys says: "We have no trace of any fairies (in Wales) approaching the minute dimensions of Shakespeare's Queen Mab, for . . . our fairies are mostly represented as not extravagantly unlike other people in personal appearance—not so unlike in fact, that other folk might not be mistaken for them now and then as late as the latter part of the fifteenth century." And a reference is made to the history of the *Gwydir* family where *David ap Jenkin* rose up against one *Howell ap Jevan ap Rys Gethin* of the castle of Dolwyddelan, "and being superior to him . . . took him in his bed . . . and brought him to Conway Castle. Thus, after many bickerings between Howell and *David ap Jenkin*, he being too weake, was faigne to flie the country, and to go to Ireland, where he was a yeare. . . . In the end he returned in the summer time, having himself, and all his followers, clad in greene . . . lurking by day, and walking in the night for feare of his adversaries; and much of the country as happened to have a sight of him and his followers, said they were fairies, and so ran away."

Chapter Six

MIXED MARRIAGES

THE marriage of young men to fairy maidens, hardly ever the other way about, was a theme of wide interest. In this group we have one or two very beautiful and romantic stories not easily matched from any other country. I will give first the oldest written version known to us, preserved by Walter Maps (*Gwallter Map*) in his *De Nugis Curialium*. The editor, in a footnote, says of these stories that "they belong to a well-known group—that of the Swan-maiden, so called because in its most mythical and barbarous form the heroine appears first as a swan or in the form of some other bird, usually aquatic, sheds her feather-robe and bird-nature, and assumes a purely human shape, in which she is captured by the hero by obtaining possession of her feathers, thus preventing her from again taking bird-form and escaping. The object of her capture is, in most of the variants, marriage, though in one group it is, primarily at all events, to learn the secret of which the heroine is the depository. . . . The marriage is assented to by the heroine upon conditions, the violation of which releases her and she flies away, to be recaptured by her husband, if at all, after long and arduous adventures.

Where the supernatural robe is part of the story, the marriage can be continued only so long as the hero retains possession of it; when the heroine recovers it she departs." In one form or another the story is known practically the world over.

Of the Welsh versions none belongs to the most primitive type, and most of them are connected with lakes. The one condition of marriage invariably being that the bride should not be hit with iron, and though in this story there is no specific mention of iron, the bridle, with which in the other versions the wives are hit, nevertheless figures. Most likely it was in the original form of this story:

"Wastin Wastiniauc (*Gwestin Gwestiniog*) they say, stayed by the lake of Brekeniauc . . . and saw on three clear moonlit nights bands of women dancing in his fields of oats, and followed them till they plunged into the water of the lake; but on the fourth night he caught one of them. Her captor also said that each night after they had plunged in he heard them murmuring beneath the water and saying 'If he had done so and so he would have caught one of us.' So he learnt from themselves the way in which he caught this one. She yielded to him and married him, also her first words to her husband were: 'I will gladly serve you and obey you with all devotion till the day when you are about to rush out at the shouting of the Levem, and strike me with your bridle.' Now Levem (*Llyfni*) is a river near the lake. This actually happened: After many children were born to him of her, she was struck with a bridle by him, and when he got back he found her fleeing with the children, followed them, and barely succeeded in catching one of his sons, Trinio."

The story proceeds to tell how the ambitious Trinio left his own estate and chose to serve the King of *Deheubarth*, how he was wounded in battle and was never seen again. It was believed in the neighbourhood that his mother rescued him and took him with her to the lake where "he still lives with her."

This is quite contrary to the general run of Welsh legends for the fairy mother usually leaves her children behind but takes her cattle with her.

There is a story told of how the son of *Hafodgarreg*, a farm in the parish of Pentrevoelas, a mountain district in west Denbigh-shire, saw through the mist, while minding his father's sheep, a lovely young girl sitting by a stack of peat. She seemed to be in great distress and was crying piteously. The young man approached her and tried to console her. She was very beautiful and as his efforts to soothe her were taken kindly and had the desired effect, he was encouraged to go further and to speak of love, which seemed to make her happier still. But while they were thus engaged, an aged and venerable looking man suddenly appeared by their side and, addressing the young girl as her father, ordered her to follow him. The young man lingered long on that spot hoping that by some chance she might return, and though he made daily visits to it they were in vain.

But they were not destined to part like this for ever, for she loved him too, and in her home "land of allurement and illusion (*hud a lledrith*) she planned a visit to the earth [to meet] her lover, but she was soon missed by her father [who] . . . came upon them . . . conversing lovingly together." A great deal of conversation passed between father and daughter, while the young man "begged and begged" of him to let her marry him. When the father perceived that the young man was in such deep earnest he turned to his daughter who, he now realised, was also deeply in love with him and asked her if she wished to marry "a man of the earth." She replied that she did, whereupon he gave his consent and told the young man that he would give them a bagful of "bright money" to start their life with, "and that she would stay with him until he struck her with iron. They were duly married, received the promised dowry, had children and lived very happily together.

One day they went to the hill to catch two ponies to take them to a church festival (the wife having now presumably become a Christian); they had got them into a corner and the farmer thought that he could at least catch one of them and was quietly approaching him, when he suddenly turned round and shot past him. In his anger he threw the bridle after him, but it was badly aimed and instead of hitting the pony hit his wife—and that meant the end of their married life together. The one condition had been violated and the marriage became automatically dissolved. Almost before they realised the tragic consequence of the accident, her father appeared on the scene with a host of fairies and took her back to her home, allowing her no time even to bid farewell to her husband or children. These—and the wealth she brought with her—were the only memorials the shepherd now had of that sweet companion who had brought so much love and happiness into his life.

Glasynys—whom the reader knows by now—has preserved a similar story for us: One morning as the son of *Ystrad* was watching his sheep on the side of *Moel Eilio*, he met a very beautiful girl. He met her several times after this and at last told his father, who "advised him to seize her the next time he saw her." This may seem a strange bit of advice to give, but one must remember that these stories are very old and may have come down to us from the time when marriage by capture was a prevalent practice. Marriage by capture was undoubtedly practised by the Welsh tribes, and the mock captures and escapes that were a feature of mounted marriages even to within living memory were a pale survival of that practice. However, not only did the father think it was the most natural advice to give, but the son also thought that it was the best thing to do, so the next time he saw her he proceeded to carry it out. Before he had got very far, however, "a little fat old man came to them and begged him to give her back to him, to which the youth would not listen. The little man uttered terrible threats, but he would not yield, so an agreement was made between them that he was to have her to wife until he touched her with iron." To the great joy of both they were soon married and lived together in great happiness for many years. But one day, "on the evening of *Bettws* Fair the wife's horse got restive, and somehow, as the husband was attending to the horse, the stirrups touched the skin of her leg, and that very night she was taken away from him." She left three or four children, and some of her descendants were known to Glasynys when he wrote the account in 1863.

But the most romantic tale is that which comes from North Wales, and has been preserved in many collections.

It concerns the son of *Upper Drws y Coed* in the parish of Beddgelert who, on calm, fine summer evenings and moonlit nights used to go out into the fields to watch the fairies dance, and listen to their music, as his own family and his neighbours had done before him many a time. One evening they came to a small field near the house and there danced, coming, as they swung round, even to the edge of the circle where he stood. They were all very beautiful but one in particular was of exceptional beauty "beyond anything he had ever seen. Her countenance was like alabaster; her voice as sweet as the voice of the nightingale and as gentle as the breeze of a summer's evening in a flower garden; her bearing was graceful and noble, and she danced as lightly on the green grass as the rays of the moon on the waters of the nearby lake. He fell in love with her over head and ears, and under the impulse of that sudden passion, when the merriment was at its height," he rushed into the ring, seized her in his strong arms and ran with her into the house.

After he had got her under his roof he tried by every means in his power to win her affection and get her to marry him, but to no avail, she would on no account consent to that; however, as she realised that he would never allow her to return to her own people, she agreed to serve him as a maid—if he could find out her name. Hiding one's name is a motif in more than one Welsh legend. The peasantry of Wales, like those of many other countries, were rather chary of giving their name to strangers, for there existed a belief amongst them that if a person could get hold of one's name he would have some power over one's life and destiny. Even today especially along the border, in the Anglicised parts of mid-Wales, you will find a decided unwillingness to reveal one's name or to put it on paper. Two hundred years ago, as we learn from the autobiography of *Twm O'r Nant*, many Welsh parents believed that if their children were sent to school they would be taken away from them because they had put their names on papers. We are not surprised, therefore, that a Welsh fairy, too, should not wish to lay herself open to all the dangers that the possession of her name would expose her to.

But to return to our young man: he tried every name known

to him but to no avail, yet he would not give up. One night as he was returning from market he saw a group of fairies in a nearby turbary who seemed to be discussing some very serious matter, and it occurred to him that they might be trying to devise some means of rescuing their sister. He thought, too, that if only he could get nearer he might find out her name. After looking carefully over the ground again he saw that a ditch ran through the turbary and passed close to where they stood. He went round to the ditch and crawled through it to within hearing distance. True enough they were discussing the fate of their lost sister, and one of them cried out sorrowfully, "O Penelope, Penelope! my sister, why did you run away with one of the mortals." "Penelope, Penelope," he echoed, "that's the name," and back he turned crawling warily lest they should see him, and reached home unobserved. When he got in he called her, "Penelope, my dear one, come here." She came, but she did not share his excitement. She lifted her clasped hands and exclaimed, "My fate! my fate! Oh, Mortal! who revealed my name to you?" She knew now her lot, and resigned herself to it, throwing herself wholeheartedly into her work. Everything she undertook prospered and there was no woman more clean or thrifty in all the land; while previously they only milked twice a day, she, according to one version, milked three times and had the same quantity as they in each of their milkings. The butter was so plentiful that nobody thought of weighing it. But the young man was not satisfied—he wanted her to be his wife and not his servant; at last, after much pleading, she consented, laying down only one condition, which was, that if he struck her with iron she should be free. He agreed and they were married. One day he wanted to go to Caernarvon Fair and went to a nearby turbary to catch a young filly, but despite his best efforts he failed. He then called Penelope to help him; she came, and they succeeded in getting her to a corner, but when he was making carefully towards her she turned and bolted once again. In his chagrin he threw the bridle after her. Alas! it was a badly aimed throw and instead of hitting the filly he hit his wife. The instant she felt the cold iron on her face she vanished, and her poor husband never saw her again, though it would seem that she was always hovering round and did not forget them, "for one cold, frosty night a very long time afterwards, he was roused from his sleep by a gentle tapping on ... his bedroom window," and he heard her voice asking him to care for the little ones and to see that they were warm:

"*Os bydd anwyd ar fy mab,*	"If my son should feel the cold,
Rhowch am dano gôb ei dad.	In his father's coat enfold.
Os bydd anwyd ar liw'r can	Should it seize my darling fair
Rhowch am dani bais ei mam."	Wrap her in my robe with care."

The descendants of this union were called *Pellings*, a corruption of the mother's name. An Anglesey man recording this story in 1802 says that the father of Lady Bulkeley was a descendant, and that "there are still living several opulent and respectable people who are known to have sprung from the Pellings. The best blood in my own veins is this Fairy's."

In my original draft I had intended to put the next two stories under the legends of the lakes—as indeed in one sense that is what they really are—but they seem to follow on so naturally here that I have now decided against it.

The first of these comes from the same district, for '*Llyn y Dywarchen* (Lake of the Sod) is immediately behind the farmhouse of *Drws y Coed Uchaf*. The name, Lake of the Sod, is rather misleading, for the "sod" was in reality a small island, on which there often grazed a number of cattle and which floated from one side of the lake to the other, according to the direction of the wind. Giraldus Cambrensis describes it in his *Itinerary Through Wales*: "On the highest parts of these mountains [Snowdonia] are two lakes worthy of admiration. The one has a floating island in it, which is often driven from one side to the other by the force of the winds; and the shepherds behold with astonishment their cattle, whilst feeding, carried to the distant parts of the lake." Local people believed that "if it floated towards the north the markets would rise, if to the south they would fall." Pennant, in his *Tours in Wales*, describing it more in detail, says that it was "about nine yards long . . . a piece of turbary, undermined by the water, torn off, and kept together by . . . the roots."—But back to our legend.

One misty day on the mountains the son of *Drws y Coed* was minding the sheep, a little below *Cwm Marchnad*, when, on crossing the wet moorland, he saw standing "in the shelter of a small tump an exceptionally beautiful little woman, her golden hair hung in curled locks, her eyes were of the blue of the clear sky . . . and a red rose on each plump cheek." The love-struck swain approached her and asked if they might talk and become friends. She extended her hand and said with a smile: "The idol of my hopes, you have come at last." After that they used to meet every day here and there on the moors. At last his love became a consuming passion that allowed him no peace, day or night. For long periods he would not be seen, and his friends believed that he was under some spell; his secret, however, came out at last, and it was discovered that the two were in the habit of meeting by some bushes near the lake, which afterwards became known as the Maiden's Grove. After a long courtship they decided to get married, but first of all they had to get her father's consent. It was arranged that they should meet on a moonlit night in the trees, but the fairy family did not appear until the moon had gone beyond the *Garn*; then they came and without any introduction or ceremony her father blurted out: "You shall have my daughter on the condition that you will not strike her with iron. If ever you touch her flesh with *that thing* she will no longer belong to you but will return to her people." Great was the young man's joy as he gave his ready consent to the condition. They were married and though nothing was said in the interview on the mountain about a dowry it was rumoured that she brought with her an enormous sum of money, so that the mountain shepherd became a rich and responsible man. In the course of time several children were born to them and everything went on happily for a number of years.

But the fatal day came! The two were out riding and happened to go near *Llyn y Gadair*, when her horse got into a bog and sank to his belly. After getting his beloved Bella (for so was she named) to safety, the horse was pulled out and freed. He then lifted her up to ride pillion behind him on his own horse, but unfortunately, as she hastened to put her foot in the stirrup-iron, it touched her knee. Before they were half-way home several of the little people had been seen, the sound of sweet music had also been heard coming from the side of the hill, and before he reached home she had vanished. It is believed that she escaped to the lake, and from there to her own home underneath. As the condition on which she was allowed to be his wife was broken, the marriage became void and she never went back to him, though some said that she and her mother, to circumvent the law of her own land, which did not permit her to walk the earth with any human being, devised a way of enabling her and her husband to meet again often: "A large piece of turf" (the detached portion of the bank, described above) "was set to float on the surface of the water, and on that she would stay for long hours, talking freely to her husband. By this means they managed to live together" until he died.

Their descendants owned *Drws y Coed* for many generations and intermarried with the people of the district, so that the men of Pennant became known as *Bellisians*, after Bella, the lake-fairy. Many a fierce fight took place between them and the men of Eifionydd in the local wakes, because they shouted "Bellisians!" after them.

But the most famous legend of all is that connected with *Llyn y Fan Fach* in the Black Mountain district of Carmarthenshire, which has been preserved for us by Mr. Rees of Tonn, a Llandovery printer, who flourished in the early part of last century. It appeared first in the introduction to his book on *The Physicians of Myddvai*, published in 1861. In the form given by Rees it is the longest and most detailed of the legends we possess, and was told him by old inhabitants from the neighbourhood of the lake: Back in the days of the Welsh princes, about the close of the twelfth century, there lived at a farm called *Blaensawdde* in the parish of Llanddeusant, Carmarthenshire, a widow whose husband had fallen in the wars of independence then waging. Despite her misfortune she seems to have prospered, so much so that her stock could not all be grazed on her own farm but had to be driven for extra pasture to the adjoining mountain.

Now this widow had a son who, when he grew up to manhood, was sent by her to look after the cattle, which seemed to favour the neighbourhood of the lake, and one day as he was walking along the margin "to his great astonishment, he beheld, sitting on the unruffled surface of the water, a lady; one of the most beautiful creatures that mortal eyes ever beheld, her hair flowed gracefully in ringlets over her shoulders, the tresses of which she arranged with a comb." Suddenly she saw the young man there on the bank—and if he wasn't offering her some of his bread and cheese!

Imperceptibly she glided towards him as he still gazed in admiration upon her and held out his hand, but she refused his offer of bread saying:

> "*Cras dy fara;*   "Hard baked is thy bread;
> *Nid hawdd fy nala.*"   'Tis not easy to catch me."

and at once dived under the waters, leaving our love-stricken swain a prey to disappointment and a sense of frustration.

When he got home he told his mother of the wonderful vision of beauty he had seen on the lake and how she had disdainfully refused his bread. She advised him to take with him next time some "unbaked dough . . . as there must have been some spell connected with the hard-baked bread." The following morning, thus extraordinarily armed to win a fair lady, he made for the mountain again—and at once for the lake—but though he watched for hours she never appeared. Then he noticed that some of the cattle were on the precipitous side of the lake, opposite, and in some danger; he rushed round towards them and to his great delight saw once again, looking more beautiful than ever, the one he had been watching so long for. He again offered her his bread, and went a stage further than the day before, in declaring his love, and uttering vows of eternal fidelity. She refused both saying:

> "*Llaith dy fara,*   "Unbaked is thy bread!
> *Ti ni fynna.*"   I will not have thee."

But he noticed that a smile played on her face as she turned away and disappeared under the waters. In a much more cheerful mood he returned home and acquainted his mother with the second

"Cras dy fara; nid hawdd fy nala"

day's events. She now suggested that he should take moderately baked bread with which to try her, and so, curiously armed again, he made for the mountain, but it proved a barren day of useless watching, until he was on the point of departing when she appeared and came towards' him. "A smile encouraged him to seize her hand, neither did she refuse the . . . bread he offered her; and after some persuasion she consented to become his bride, on condition that they should only live together until she received from him . . . *tri ergyd diachos*—three causeless blows." After this she darted into the lake, presumably to break the good news to her family, for very soon there "emerged out of the lake *two* most beautiful ladies, accompanied by a hoary-headed man of noble mien and extraordinary stature, but having otherwise all the force and strength of youth." He addressed the bewildered youth in a kindly manner, saying that as he wished to marry one of his daughters, he was quite willing, provided he could say "which of the two ladies before him was the object of his affections." It was difficult if not impossible for him to tell, for they were as alike as two peas, but while he was narrowly eyeing them, one of them pushed her foot slightly forward. "The motion, simple as it was, did not escape . . . the youth, and he discovered a trifling variation in the mode with which their sandals were tied . . . for he . . . had . . . noticed . . . the peculiarity of her shoe-tie [and] he boldly took hold of her hand."

"Thou hast chosen rightly," said her father. "Be to her a kind and faithful husband, and I will give her, as a dowry, as many sheep, cattle, goats and horses as she can count of each without heaving or drawing in her breath. But remember, that if you prove unkind to her at any time, and strike her three times without a cause, she shall return to me, and shall bring all her stock back with her." Such was the verbal marriage settlement.

Then the young lady began to count, "and adopted the mode of counting by *fives*, thus: One, two, three, four, five—One, two, three, four, five; as many times as possible in rapid succession, till her breath was exhausted." She did the same in the case of the goats, cattle and horses, "and in an instant the full number of each came out of the lake when called upon by her father."

MIXED MARRIAGES

After their marriage they went to live at a farm called *Esgair Llaethdy* where they lived happily and prosperously for many years and became the parents of three sons. But as yet none of the "three causeless blows" had been given. One day, however, on the occasion of a christening to which the two were invited, the wife seemed reluctant to go, alleging that the distance was too much. Her husband told her to go and fetch one of the horses. "I will," said she, "if you will bring me my gloves which I left in our house." He went, but on returning and finding that she had not moved "he jocularly slapped her shoulder with one of them saying 'go! go!' [*dôs! dôs!*], when she reminded him of the understanding upon which she consented to marry him . . . and warned him to be more cautious for the future."

On another occasion, when they both made up a party of merry and hilarious guests at a wedding, she suddenly burst into tears "and sobbed most piteously." Her husband "touched her on the shoulder" and asked her why she was crying. She replied: "Now people are entering into trouble, and your troubles are likely to commence, as you have the *second* time stricken me without a cause."

Both now realised how careful they had to be; there remained but one blow more and it could be so easily given in a jocular or forgetful moment. She assured him that she loved him dearly and prayed that nothing might happen to separate them, happy as they were in each other's life and in the lives of their brilliant and dutiful children. "It, however, so happened that one day they were together at a funeral, where . . . she appeared to be in the highest and gayest of spirits and indulged in immoderate fits of laughter, which so shocked her husband that he touched her, saying, 'Hush! hush! don't laugh.' She said she laughed 'because people when they die go out of trouble,' and rising up, she went out of the house, saying 'The last blow has been struck, our marriage contract is broken, and at an end! Farewell'." Then she made for *Esgair Llaethdy* and called all her cattle together and led them towards the lake:

"*Mu wlfrech, Moelfrech,*	"Brindled cow, white speckled,
Mu olfrech, Gwynfrech,	Spotted cow, bold freckled,

80

Pedair cae tonn-frech,	The four field sward mottled,
Yr hen wynebwen,	The old white-faced,
A'r las Geigen.	And the grey Geigen,
Gyda'r tarw gwyn	With the white Bull
O lys y Brenin;	From the court of the king;
A'r llo du bach	And the little black calf
Sydd ar y bach	Tho' suspended on the hook,
Dere dithau yn iach adre!"	Come thou also, quite well home."

It happened to be the spring of the year and four of the oxen were ploughing in one of the fields; these she also called:

"Pedwar eidion glas	"The four grey oxen
Sydd ar y maes,	That are on the field,
Deuwch chwithau	Come you also
Yn iach adre!"	Quite well home!"

And away they went after her in one long line towards the lake, 6 miles away, and disappeared beneath the waters, leaving no trace behind them "except a well-marked furrow" made by the plough the oxen dragged after them, "and which remains to this day as a testimony to the truth of the story."

Nothing further is told of the husband, but of the sons it is stated that they often went to the lake in the hope of once again seeing their mother. One day they were rewarded; quite suddenly she appeared at a place called *Llidiard y Meddygon* (The Physicians' Gate), and addressing *Rhiwallon*, the eldest, told him that his work and mission on earth was to heal the sick "for which purpose she furnished him with a bag full of medical prescriptions and instructions." She met them again on several occasions and revealed to them the medicinal qualities of the various herbs that grew on the mountainside. In time they became the best-known physicians in Wales, "and in order that their knowledge should not be lost, they wisely committed the same to writing. *Rhys Gryg*—the son of the famous *Rhys ap Tewdwr*, Prince of South Wales—appointed them court physicians, and bestowed upon them ranks, privileges and lands. These lands and farms, perpetuating their names and calling—*Llwyn Ifan Feddyg*, The Grove of Evan the Physician, and *Llwyn Meredydd Feddyg*,

The Grove of Meredith the Physician—remained in the possession of their descendants until the last century. The last to practise at Myddfai were "David Jones, of Mothvey, Surgeon," and "John Jones, Surgeon," but the last of the famous line known to practise medicine was Doctor C. Rice Williams, of Aberystwyth, who was alive in 1881.

This story of the lady of *Llyn y Fan Fach* will be the last example given of that group which tells of the marriage of *mortals* with fairies. It is a considerable group, in which North and South Wales figure. In some of the unions the fairy bride is not said to have come from a lake but to have returned to one, neither is it made clear in every case that, when touched with iron, she vanishes into one. The one feature common to them all is the warning that, should they be touched with iron, the women will return to the bosom and protection of the fairy family. It is with considerable surprise therefore that we find in the above story the substitution for it of the "three needless blows."

Usually the accident happens when they are trying to catch a horse and the fatal touch is made by some of the irons belonging to the riding tackle, generally the bridle. In the Llyn y Fan legend the hitting or "touching" is there, and catching a horse enters into it, but there is no mention of iron! Has anything gone wrong here? But then am I demanding of these ancient stories a uniformity and an agreement which I have already condemned as being one of the temptations to be withstood by every collector?

This lonely tarn high up in the Black Mountains filled quite a big place in the life and imagination of the surrounding villages and parishes. Llywelyn Williams in his book '*Slawer Dydd* refers to the great concourse that visited it on the first Sunday in August, for on that day (first Monday according to some) "a commotion took place in the lake and . . . its waters boiled, which was to herald the approach of the lake-lady and her Oxen." These excursions from districts as far apart as the Tawe and Towy valleys "in carts, gambos and all kinds of vehicles to . . . see the water nymph" continued to be popular up to the end of the last century. The "lady," whose lower part resembled "that of a dolphin, while the upper part was that of a beautiful lady," made her appearance on this Sunday and combed her hair on the reflecting surface of the placid lake.

There was more than one version of this legend, as one might expect in so romantic a story, one which would be often listened to and often repeated, thereby providing for the teller of an inventive turn of mind an opportunity of practising his gift. One version, copied by Wirt Sikes, appeared in the *Cambro-Briton*, vol. ii, p. 313 (not 315 as given by Sikes) (1821). The author, signing himself *Siencyn ab Tydvil, Trehomer*, simply says of it that it was "an unwritten tradition afloat in Carmarthenshire." It differs in many parts from Rees's version: The young man is said to have bought some lambs in a neighbouring fair and taken them to graze near *Llyn y Fan Fach*, out of which, whenever he visited them, three beautiful maidens appeared to him. He tried to catch them, but they always reached the lake before him, from the complete security of which they taunted him:

"*Cras dy fara,*   "Your bread is dry [or hard baked]
Anhawdd ein dala."   It is not easy to catch us."

Bread seems to play an important part in this legend; it was only after partaking of bread that parley took place. In one version, after the lake-fairy had partaken of the young man's bread; in this, after he had eaten some moist bread which they had sent ashore. The following day he chased them again; whether or not he derived any extra pep from eating their bread, he, however, to his great delight, managed to catch one of them. The consequent conversation moved on at a rapid pace and before it was over he had proposed, and had been accepted—if the following day he could distinguish her from her sisters. The story now follows in the main the version given above, except that the three light blows were given on one and the same occasion, but they were sufficient to make void the marriage contract and she returned with her cattle to the lake—seven cows, two oxen and one bull.

A similar story, so similar that there is no point in giving it here, is connected with *Llyn y Forwyn* in the parish of Ystrad Dyfodwg, Glamorgan, and is given by "Cadrawd" in the

Cyfaill yr Aelwyd a'r Frythones. In this, three quarrels are substituted for the three blows.

Another variant exists, making no mention of the *Meddygon,*
and with a highly coloured account of the meeting, in which a
golden-haired damsel is seen rowing on the lake in a golden boat
with a golden oar. She was first seen at midnight in the first hour
of the new year, but was shy and rowed immediately away. A
wise man advised the youth to tempt her with bread and cheese,
and from midsummer eve till the end of the year he kept daily
watch, making generous offerings of bread and cheese. Then on
the anniversary of the day he saw her first, he went up to the lake
again, with mounting hope, armed with seven loaves and a big
round cheese. At midnight he dropped them into the lake and
was soon rewarded, for she was seen coming in her magic skiff;
nor was she any longer shy, but coming ashore, promised to
marry him. All the other incidents are identical. Sir John Rhys's
comment on this version is: "Mr. Sikes . . . seems not to have
been too anxious to leave anybody the means of testing his work."

It has been said that there is no need to make any great
distinction between lake maidens and mermaids.

The coasts of Caernarvonshire and north Pembrokeshire seem
to have been noted for their stories of mermaids. The following
comes from St. Dogmael's (Llandudoch) near Cardigan: "One
fine afternoon in September, at the beginning of the last century,
a fisherman of the name of Pergrin went to a recess in a rock near
Pen Cemmaes, where a mermaid was combing her hair, and took
her a prisoner into his boat . . . We do not know what language
they speak . . . but this one, this time at any rate, is said to have
spoken splendid Welsh."

Weeping copiously and despairing of getting her freedom
again, she shouted, "Pergrin, if you will let me go, I will give
three shouts when you need them most," and so in some fear, and
wonder, too, he released her. Days passed, weeks passed, and
Pergrin never saw her again, but on another fine afternoon, when
the sea was calm, she showed her head and shouted three times.
"Pergrin! Pergrin! Pergrin! take up your nets, take up your nets,
take up your nets!" Pergrin and his companion did so immediately

and rowed back; by the time they reached a place called *Pwll Cam*, the storm had broken. The other eighteen who had gone out with them lost their lives. The men of Nefyn (Caernarvonshire) were most indignant when they found that the men of Llandudoch claimed the mermaid, maintaining that she belonged to them.

Another was seen between St. Davids and Fishguard, by some quarry-men; she, too, could speak Welsh, though the only utterance they had from her before she plunged back again into the sea was "Reaping in Pembrokeshire and weeding in Carmarthenshire" ("*medi yn Sir Benfro a chwynnu yn Sir Gâr*").

It is interesting to note that Drayton in his *Battaile of Agincourt* ascribes to the county of Cardigan the following armorial bearings:

> As Cardigan the next to them that went,
> Came with a mermayd sitting on a rock.

Chapter Seven

LEGENDS OF THE LAKES

ARGE number of legends centre round Llangorse Lake in Breconshire. It goes by various names: Brecknock Mere, *Llyn Safaddan*, Talyllyn Pool and Llangorse Lake. Lying in a hollow about 6 miles south-east of the county town, it is the largest sheet of fresh water in South Wales and is about 2 miles long and 1 wide. The River *Llyfni*, which rises in the hills to the south, flows past the ancient castle of *Blaenllyfni* and the church of Llangasty Talyllyn, and, after passing right through the lake, flows out at the other end to join the Wye at Glasbury.

We owe the preservation of one story to our friend, Giraldus Cambrensis: "The famous lake of Brecheinoc supplies the country with pike, perch, excellent trout, tench and eels. A circumstance concerning this lake, which happened a short time before our days, must not be passed over in silence. In the reign of King Henry I, Gruffydd, son of Rhys ap Tewdwr, held under the King one comot . . . in the *Cantref Mawr*, which, in title and

"Prince Gruffydd and the Birds"

dignity, was esteemed by the Welsh equal to the Southern part of Wales, called *Deheubarth* . . . When Gruffydd, on his return from the king's court, passed near this lake, which at that cold season of the year was covered with water fowl of various sorts, being accompanied by Milo, earl of Hereford, and Lord of Brecheinoc, and Payn Fitz-John, Lord of Ewyas, who were at that time secretaries and privy counsellors to the king. Earl Milo, wishing to draw forth from Gruffydd some discourse concerning his innate nobility, rather jocularly than seriously thus addressed him: 'It is an ancient saying in Wales that if the natural prince of the country, coming to this lake, shall order the birds to sing they will immediately obey.' To which Gruffydd, richer in mind than in gold (for though his inheritance was diminished, his ambition and dignity still remained), answered: 'Do you, therefore, who now hold the dominion of this land first give the command.' But he and Payn having in vain commanded, and Gruffydd perceiving that it was necessary for him to do so in his turn, dismounted from his horse, and falling on his knees towards the east, as if he had been about to engage in battle, prostrate on the ground, with his eyes and hands uplifted to heaven, poured forth devout prayers to the Lord; at length, rising up, and signing his face and forehead with the figure of the cross, he thus openly spake: 'Almighty God, and Lord Jesus Christ, who knowest all things, declare here this day thy power. If thou hast caused me to descend lineally from the natural princes of Wales, I command these birds in thy name to declare it,' and immediately the birds, beating the water with their wings, began to cry aloud, and to proclaim him. The spectators were astonished and confounded; and Earl Milo hastily returning with Payn Fitz-John to court, related this singular occurrence to the king who is said to have replied: 'By the death of Christ (an oath he was accustomed to use) it is not a matter of so much wonder; for although by our great authority we commit acts of violence and wrong against these people, yet they are known to be the rightful inheritors of the land'." Giraldus further says of this lake: "it is sometimes seen by the inhabitants covered and adorned with buildings, pastures, gardens and orchards."

I suppose the most famous lake legend is that which tells how the *Ychen Bannog* of *Hu Gadarn* dragged the *afanc* out of the lake. It is preserved in a letter of Edward Llwyd, dated 1693, in the possession of Canon Robert Williams of *Rhyd y Croesau*, which he sent to the *Cambrian Journal* in 1859. This does not profess to be an exact transcription; I have used with it the version given in D. E. Jenkins's *Beddgelert*.

It would seem that the inhabitants of the Conway Valley were sorely troubled by the existence in the river, not far from Bettws y Coed, of a monster which caused disastrous floods in the district. Many attempts had been made to destroy him; but neither arrow, spear nor dart made the least impression upon him. They realised, therefore, that the only thing to do with him was to drag him out of the lake. That might be accomplished, but there remained another problem—what to do with him when they got him out, for a creature like that could not be allowed to roam about the countryside at will. That, too, was solved, and they decided to take him to another lake, higher up in Snowdonia, *Llyn Ffynnon Las*, beyond their own watershed, in *Cwm Dyli*.

Next, strong iron chains were forged and two of the mightiest oxen in the kingdom—the long-horned oxen of *Hu Gadarn*, reputed to be the twin calves of the famous Freckled Cow—were secured. A damsel is said to have enticed him out of the lake and while he went to sleep with his head upon her knee advantage was taken of it to bind him with the chains. When he woke up and saw the trick that had been played upon him, he rushed back into the lake, horribly mutilating the girl, probably in revenge for her part in luring him away from safety. Fortunately for the people they had now the chains round him and more fortunately still these proved long enough to be hitched to the oxen, which then began to show the power of their mighty frames as they gradually brought him to shore. It would seem that some of the people did all they could to help them and began now to brag about it, each maintaining that he pulled harder than anybody else. This was more than the *afanc* could stand—he knew very well where the power came from, and is said to have answered them:

"Oni bae y dai ag a dyn   "Had it not been for the oxen
                                           pulling,

Ni ddaetha'r afanc byth o'r llyn."   The afanc had never left the
                                           pool."

The oxen now dragged him through the parish of Dolwyddelen "and through the pass, which has ever since been called *Bwlch Rhiw yr Ychain* (The Hilly Pass of the Oxen) . . . They next reached one of the mountain fields of *Gwastad Annas*; and it was in this field that one of the oxen dropped its eye through exertion . . . This field has been called, on that account, *Gwaen Llygad yr Ych* (The Field of the Ox's Eye). The pain which the ox suffered . . . was so great that it wept copiously, and its tears made a pool which is even now called *Pwll Llygad yr Ych* (The Pool of the Ox's Eye)."

With immense exertion and labour the *afanc* was drawn up through *Cwm Dyli*, as far as *Llyn Ffynnon Las* where, as the chains were loosed, the monster jumped headlong into the lake.

The people of *Cwm Dyli* did not mind having the monster in their lake at all, for it already had an unenviable reputation as the abode of creatures as bad as he, "and it was only fitting that he should be permitted to go to his kind." The *afanc* had learnt no lesson but began his *afancish* tricks right away; he killed all the fish, caused furious commotion in the waters, and woe betide any creature that fell into the lake.

"There was in Wales as late as the close of the seventeenth century a strange piece of music, known to many, which was an imitation of the lowing of oxen, and clanking of chains heard while the *Avanc* was being drawn from the lake. It was called 'Cainc yr Ychain Banawg' [Lay of the Bannog Oxen]."

Sir John Rhys has some interesting comments to make on water spirits and divinities, amongst whom he would put the *afanc* who, whatever may be made of him, yet speaks the language of the country. He sees also in this story, where the *afanc* has caused floods, the echo of "some such a local legend which has been generalised into a sort of universal flood story in a late Triad. Three masterpieces of the Isle of *Prydain*: The Ship of *Nefydd Naf Neifion*, that carried in her male and female of every kind when the Lake of Llion burst; and Hu the Mighty's *Ychen Bannog* dragging the *afanc* of the lake to land, so that the lake burst no more . . ."

In this connexion it is interesting to note what D. E. Jenkins, in his book, *Beddgelert*, says of *Bryn Diweddu* (the Hill of the Finishing) near Llyn Dinas, that it was so called "because it was here they used to finish up the ceremonies connected with the drawing of the *afanc* out of the lake. This happened on the first of May, and was done as a commemorating service of the Flood, and the saving of Noah and his family in the ark. The proceedings were carried on something in this way: At the upper end of the lake a kind of a large ferry-boat was built; it was then covered over with green clods and leafy boughs, to represent the earth. On the first of May, a man and a woman were placed in the boat, and were given the name of *Dwyf* and *Dwyfan* (the God and the Goddess); then the immense oxen called *Ychain Bannog* . . . were chained to it, and pulled it down to the lower end of the lake. It was there pulled safely to land, amid the greatest rejoicings of the spectators. The oxen were then released from the boat and led to the top of the mound, where they were slaughtered as a sacrifice. Then, as soon as the sacrifice began to burn, immense bonfires were made on the mountain-tops, as a sign to the whole country that sacrificing was going on. This is the origin of the burning of gorse on the evening of the first of May."

The story of the dragging of a monster out of a lake comes from many districts and seems to be as common as the belief that lakes were brought into existence to drown some wicked Sodom or Gomorrah in the plains or in the valleys. It is connected with *Llyn yr Wyth Eidon* (the Lake of the Eight Oxen) in Anglesey. *Hu Gadarn* is represented here as needing eight oxen for the task and not two. The same is said of *Llyn Barfog*, but by King Arthur's horse and not by *Hu's* oxen. It is connected also with Llangorse Lake where it would appear the *afanc* was taken away "from the lake in a cart or waggon drawn by oxen."

The majority of the lake legends are tales of vengeance. In nearly all cases they are supposed to have come into existence to avenge the wickedness of a town or a ruling potentate and nearly all exhibit a dull and drab sameness; occasionally one gets here and there a minor twist which is a welcome relief. Davies, in his *Mythology of the British Druids*, says that "the annotator upon Camden mentions the names of six lakes in which ancient cities are reported to have been drowned" and adds that he himself could supply several others to the list. He then goes on to give the legend of Llangorse Lake "as related to him by an old man in the town of Hay": "The site of the present lake was formerly occupied by a very large city, but the inhabitants were reported to be very wicked. The king of the country sent his servant to examine into the truth of the rumour, adding a threat that in case it should prove to be well founded, he would destroy the place, as an example to his other subjects." The royal representative arrived in the town in the evening and found all the inhabitants engaged in riotous festivity. Not one of them took the least notice of the stranger or offered him hospitality. In a mean habitation he, however, found one open door through which he entered, only to find that the family had gone to the festivities, all but the baby, whom he found weeping in his cradle. He sat down by the little innocent and tried to soothe him, grieving at the thought that he, too, must perish with the rest of the wicked town. In this situation he spent the night and while endeavouring to amuse the child, accidentally dropped one of his gloves into the cradle. The next morning, before daybreak, he departed to report the sad truth to the king.

"He had just left the town when he heard a noise behind him, like a tremendous crack of thunder mixed with dismal shrieks and lamentations. He stopped to listen. Now it sounded like the lashing of waves: and presently all was dead silence." As it was still dark he could not see what had happened; he, however, decided to pursue his journey, but as the morning was cold he looked for his gloves and finding only one he remembered that the other had fallen into the cradle. As they were a present from the king he felt he ought not to return without them, so he went back. But when he got to the place where the town ought to be, he saw no buildings at all, just one vast sheet of water, and as he gazed on the desolate scene he saw in the middle of the lake a tiny object which the wind was gently wafting towards him. When it came near he recognised it as the cradle in which he had left his glove; in it, too, was the little innocent "alive and unhurt" whom he carried to the King—the one single soul saved out of that wretched place.

In one of the versions the inundation is said to have come as a judgment upon a wicked prince who neither feared God nor regarded man, but who, despite warnings and protests, persisted in his career of blasphemy, openly scorning religion and the teaching of Holy Church. Sorrow, which would have softened the hearts of most—his only son died—only hardened him in his evil ways. On the very night of the funeral, he held a great feast in which he and his choice friends abandoned themselves to all excesses. Heaven struck at last. Peals of thunder were heard, crashing with deafening violence; the earth heaved up and broke in twain. Through this gap the River *Llyfni* swept in and the palace was swallowed up. No soul was saved. And because of the wickedness of this Lord of *Llyfni* and *Safaddan*, the waters of the *Llyfni* as they pass through will not mix with the water of the lake.

In a variant of the above, the wicked prince is said to have been cruel and extortionate and to have been warned by "a voice" many a time. He, too, made a great feast and summoned two bards to entertain his guests. When the midnight bell tolled the solemn hour a loud clap of thunder shook the whole place and the voice was heard for the last time: "Vengeance is come!" The two minstrels, looking in the direction the voice came from, saw "a hand beckoning them to follow"; before they had gone very far they heard loud screams and the noise of many waters!

The same story is told of *Llyn Tegid*, or Bala Lake, in North Wales. The same wicked prince, the same warning voice, "Vengeance will come!" To celebrate the birth of his son and heir, he makes a great feast, and invites a harper to entertain his guests. At midnight the harper hears a voice whispering to him, "Vengeance, vengeance." He turns and sees, not a hand, but a little bird, beckoning him. Some distance outside he stops, and thinking that he has been foolish, tries to return, but is completely lost.

In the morning he sees no trace of the palace but a large sheet of water, and his harp floating on it.

There is another version of the legend, but since it is practically identical with that connected with Kenfig Pool, I will give it as related of the latter. But first of all a word about Kenfig, for its story is far more romantic than any legend. Travellers by the mail train from London to Fishguard know very well the dreary aspect of this stretch between Pyle and Port Talbot: for the most part it is wet and flat and broken up into sand dunes, producing a coarse herbage on which a few cattle and many ponies graze. It was once a fair land of green meadows much like that of the lowland hundred inundated by the sea, but it was the sand that inundated the land of Kenfig, so that we have here not only the legend of a buried city, but the history of a buried town. Much land has been lost to the sea and the sand between Gower and the mouth of the River Ogmore. Many references to storms, devastations and loss of grazing land are met with in the correspondence of Margam Abbey, to which the original manor of Kenfig was given, in 1147, by Robert of Caen, Lord of *Tir Iarll* and founder of the abbey.

It had suffered terribly when Leland visited it in 1540: "A village on the est side of Kenfik and a castel, both in ruines and almost shokid and devourid with the sandes," but the most disastrous visitation was that which in 1607 overwhelmed the town and piled up the sand over the whole area—here we have legend and history walking side by side.

How vastly and incredibly changed is the scene today! On the sand dunes, on piles and pillars driven deep into the earth, has been constructed the biggest and most modern steel works in the British Isles, indeed, anywhere in the world outside America. A whole town has been built to house the workers, making some amends to ancient Kenfig—but they are still troubled by the sand, which sweeps round the houses and in at the windows and under the doors.

Nearby is the Kenfig Pool, which occupies an area of about 70 acres, and though it is only 1,000 yards from the sea there is no trace of salt water in it.

That briefly is the history; here is the legend: "A peasant's son loved the daughter of the Lord of Clare" but she would not have him because he was poor, so he took to the highway to watch the agent of the lord of the district returning with the lord's rents. "He killed him and took the money, and showed her the coin and the lady married him; he then made a magnificent feast and invited the chief men of the country to it. . . . The second night, the marriage took place, and when they were merriest, a voice was heard . . . 'Vengeance will come! Vengeance will come! Vengeance will come!' three times. And they asked when. 'At the end of the ninth generation,' said the voice. 'There is no occasion for us to fear,' said they, 'all of us will be under the earth long before that.' Nevertheless, they lived till a descendant was born of the ninth generation; and another, a descendant of the man that was killed, seeing the arrival of that period, visited Cynfig (Kenfig), a young man, discreet and comely . . . and looking at the town and its wealth, without anyone possessing a furrow or corner excepting the descendants of the murderer, and he himself still living, and his wife.

"At the crowing of the cock they heard a voice. 'Vengeance is come! Vengeance is come! Vengeance is come!' 'On whom is it come?' said they. 'On him who slew my ancestor of the ninth generation.' They rose in terror and went towards the town, and there was nothing to be seen but a large lake, and in it above the surface of the water three chimney tops smoking, and the smoke of an offensive smell." Also on the water, and floating towards the young man, a pair of gloves on which, when he picked them up, he saw the name and arms of the murdered man. "And with the dawn there were countless voices praising God with heavenly songs. And thus it ends."

Upon reading closely again the Welsh version as applied to Llangorse Lake, and scraping away the preaching and the moralising, I noted a few differences that ought to be mentioned: The same poor peasant and rich heiress are there; the peasant kills and robs a carrier and says he has now plenty of money. She insists on knowing how he got it; he tells her and shows her the knife. But since some spirit was beginning to disturb the spot where the murdered man was buried, she insisted on his going to the grave to appease his ghost and to hear what he had to say. When there, he heard a voice crying: "Is there no vengeance for innocent blood?" and another answering: "No, not till the ninth generation." Then it proceeds in much the same way except that on the arrival of a child of that generation they make a great feast, in the midst of which vengeance falls, leaving nothing but the waters of the *Safaddan*!

It will be noted that the minstrels invariably escape, and that there is generally something floating on the waters—a harp, a pair of gloves, or a cradle.

A rather curious legend is connected with Crumlyn or *Crymlyn* Lake which is said to cover the old town of Swansea: St. Patrick returning to his native land is abused near this spot by his fellow-countrymen for leaving it. St. Patrick being a quick-tempered Welshman could not stand this sort of treatment, so "he caused his vilifiers to be transformed into fishes; but some of them, being females, were converted into fairies instead." The sun never shines on it except for one week in the whole year. It had another peculiarity: "It was said that should any person happen to stand with his face towards the lake when the wind is blowing across the lake, and that if any of the spray of that water should touch his clothes, it would be only with the greatest difficulty he could save himself from being attracted or sucked into the water." The writer goes on to explain the working of this sympathetic magic: "The spray which wets his clothes, however little, was evidently regarded as establishing a link of connexion between him and the body of the water—or shall I say rather, between him and the divinity of the water?—and that this link was believed to be so strong that it required the man's utmost effort to break it and escape being drawn in and drowned."

There is another lake, *Llyn Llynclys* (the lake of the swallowed court) of great depth, in the neighbourhood of Oswestry, about which there is a legend in which the vengeance takes a more subtle turn—here, the schemer himself is caught in the coils of his own machinations and his punishment begins at once. The lake has, besides, the usual legend of the wicked ruler, the warning

97

voice, the feast, the catastrophe, and the floating harp of the escaped minstrel.

The other legend has been often told under various titles: "The Swallowed Court"; "The Maid of the Green Forest"; "The Lady of the Lake," etc. The author of the verses embodying the legend, John F. M. Dovaston, was a local poet, and the verses were published by him, along with others, in 1825. How much comes from genuine local tradition and how much from Dovaston's poetic imagination it is impossible to say, he at any rate belonged to the district. Like others after him he is supposed to have created his own names for the characters—Alaric for the king—and why not? it is as good as any, and its three short syllables weave themselves easily into the fabric of the verses and fall trippingly off the tongue. For the clerk's name he has used a local place-name (Willin, an Anglicised form of Wylan) from *Croes Wylan* (Wylan's Cross). Connected with so ancient a monument, it may, of course, be the original name in the legend:

King Alaric was getting tired of his wife's faded beauty; while he was still young she had become wrinkled and shrunken with "rheumy eyes," and he hated the very sight of her. Then one day when he was out hunting in the "green forest" there came up to him a maiden of overpowering beauty who appeared to be as anxious, after only this brief encounter, to be his wife as he was to make her his queen.

> By my side each day rode this lady gay,
> And sweetly thus she sang:
>
> Oh, take me to thy fair palace,
> Oh, take me for thy queen,
> And racy wine shall then be thine
> As never a man has seen.
>
> And never shall fail thy rich banquet,
> And my beauty no change shall know,
> Till within thy hall the flag-reeds tall,
> And the long green rushes grow.

*

But ere I become thy wedded wife
Thou a solemn oath must make,
And let hap whate'er thou must not dare
That solemn oath to break.

That to leave thy bed unfollowed
To me 'tis freely given;
And that none shall enquire where I retire
One night in every seven.

Having eagerly agreed to this condition the king returned to the palace to perform a very disagreeable business, and that was to tell the hag with the "rheumy eyes" that a very attractive and beautiful young maiden was going to take her place, but when he got there he found to his surprise, and relief, that she was nowhere to be found, and he never saw her again.

As the years went by he became more and more troubled about the disappearance one night in seven of his young queen—where was she going, what was she doing? And he pours out his heart before Willin, his trusted clerk:

Oh, sad and dark, thou learned Clerk,
Is my life with sorrow riven,
And thus I am doomed with grief to be gloomed
One night in every seven

★

But what she does, or where she goes,
I dare not ask to know.

And though she has been all night abroad
In a thin, loose night-robe dressed,
Oh, strange to be told, she is nothing cold,
But glows with warmth increased.

The poor trusting Alaric did not know the true character of his clerk and chaplain, who seems to have been a monk of the "White Minster" nearby, nor could he have guessed that the clerk had cast envious eyes at his youthful wife. But Willin was not only

a shrewd and ambitious man, he was also skilled in the black art
and had schemes not only of lifting the trouble from his master's
mind but also of relieving him of the cause of it all, namely, his
young queen.

> Then Clerk Willin he cried to the troubled king,
> "Thy peace I can repair,
> If each year from your field ten beeves thou'lt yield
> To the monks of the White Minster.
>
> And peace shall preside in this fair palace,
> And thy bed with peace be blest,
> If to me thou'lt resign with her racy wine,
> The maid of the Green Forest.
>
> For I can by a spell, that I dare not tell,
> Relieve thy fettered fate;
> And I showed the young queen my powers, I ween,
> By a sign that I dare not repeat."
>
> The king cheerfully agreed and promised:
> Each year on the monks (to) bestow
> The tenth of what fed in his palace' green mead,
> And of what in his vaults did flow.
>
> Then Clerk Willin he took his clasped book,

★

> And arrived soon, ere set the moon
> On the rocks of the Giant's Grave.

He there entered a cavern "which led down to the Fairy
land," where he prepared the powerful spells that were to bring
him such a coveted prize, and the monastery the abundance of
so rich a fare.

But unfortunately the queen was also in the same cave to
undergo her weekly rejuvenation, for the secret must now be
told. The youthful queen, the Maid of the Green Forest, was in
reality the old rheumy-eyed queen. When she discovered that her

100

looks had faded and that she was losing her husband's love and affection, she decided on a hazardous step, and that was to enter into a compact with the devil that in return for the repossession of all her youthful charm she would consent to come to the cave one night in every seven and be an ogress.

> And while she was in did the Clerk begin
> His spells of potent skill;
> While the rising blast sighed low as it passed
> Through the stunted bush on the hill.

He again went carefully through the list of his requirements: peace to Alaric's board and bed; for the monks of White Minster, ten beeves from his fields and a tithe of the wine from his cellars, but for himself:

> That his queen so fine be ever mine,
> And no change let her form betide,
> But through all her years be as now appears,
> And ne'er let her leave my side.

Determined to wed her that very night at *Croes Wylan*, he summoned the spirits to produce her there:

> . . . ere glimpse of morn
> And I'll meet her and wed her there.

*

> And then as he swore, his Book he tore,
> And hastened away from the cave.

When he came to *Croes Wylan*, he became alarmed—had something gone wrong!—for there he saw,

> . . . by the light of the torches bright,
> That strange spirits there did hold
> An ogress grim that smiled at him,
> And her rheumy eyeballs rolled.

Yes, a terrible thing had happened, their spells had clashed! Before she had reached the first stage in the process of rejuvenation, he had demanded of the spirits that she should be "through all her years as she now appears"—and there she was!

Quite heartlessly she told him that he would have to take her now as she was. There was nothing either of them could do about it.

> Our power is passed, our spells have clashed,
> No charm can our fate redress,
> And a penitent now for life art thou,
> And I a grim ogress.

> On her wrinkled chin stood the grey hairs thin,
> And she close did her skin-lips squeeze;
> And thick on her brow did the grey hairs grow,
> Like the moss of old orchard trees.

She reached to the Clerk her bony finger, and continued:

> Oh, take me to thy cloistered bed,
> To be thy bosom guest,
> As by oath and spell decreed.
> And nought be thy fare but the pike and the dare,
> And the water in which they feed.

And down they all went:

> . . . the king, and his palace and all,
> And the waters now o'er it flow,
> And already in his hall do the flag-reeds tall
> And the long green rushes grow.

Natives say that when the lake is clear they can see the towers of the palace beneath. The story as told here does not possess the dramatic unity usual in such legends: the king, the central figure in the first part, gives place in the second to Clerk Willin, and disappears from the story. The punishment he is made to share in the end with his clerk does not seem to be really merited, and as no attempt has been made in the narrative to prepare us for it we are left with the feeling that he has been rather unjustly treated. Not even the final and complete retribution that the clerk draws down upon himself reconciles us to the undeserved fate of the king.

For some interesting comments upon this legend and a comparison with Fouqué's celebrated romance see *Y Cymmrodor* (1884) Vol. VII, Pt. I, p. 31.

A rather curious legend is attached to *Llyn Gwernan*, a small mountain tarn on the heights of Cadair Idris. A green man who spent his time watching the visitors who came up was said to have his home in it. When they were far up the mountain he shouted, "The hour is come. The hour is come," and brought down on them the mists and the storms, while his cry reverberated from height to height. As they lost their way in the mists and fell over the precipices to their doom, he gathered up their bodies and took them back with him to the bottom of the lake.

Chapter Eight

LEGENDS OF THE CAVES

THESE come from all parts of Wales and vary considerably in their details and motifs, making exact classification difficult. It will continue to be a difficulty right to the end, but one is in good company: Sir John Rhys, speaking of a group of legends, says, "They are difficult to classify," and of others, they "are so miscellaneous as to baffle any attempt to characterise them generally and briefly." Some could equally well be put under "hidden treasures," "sleeping warriors," "wells" or even "lakes." King Arthur is the chief figure in some of them, *Owen Lawgoch* in others.

Through the legend of the sleeping hero and his warriors—possibly the first legend I ever heard—King Arthur became an early hero of mine, so early that I was young enough to believe that he and his knights might be sleeping under the fields of our farm, and more than once I tried to see if there was an entrance in the face of the rocks that formed the precipitous sides of the wooded *cwm* encircling the bottom fields. His name was further made familiar to me as it was connected with the many standing stones in the neighbourhood—I knew of more than one *Coitan Arthur* (Arthur's Quoit).

The majority of these legends come from South Wales and the following was said to be "popular in Glamorganshire": "A Welshman walking over London Bridge with a neat hazel staff in his hand, was accosted by an Englishman, who asked him whence he came." The Welshman not liking the question answered in a somewhat brusque manner, "I am from my own country." The Englishman was clearly not familiar with our more round-about Welsh way of broaching a subject, which in this case would more likely be, in order to inspire confidence and awaken pride: "That's a fine stick you've got, Taffy." He, however, realised that he had been too brusque and asked him not to take it amiss: "If you will only answer my questions, and take my advice, it will be of greater benefit to you than you imagine. That stick in your hand grew on a spot under which are hid vast treasures of gold and silver, and if you remember the place, and conduct me to it, I will put you in possession of that treasure."

Mention of vast treasures of gold and silver made all the difference, for the Welshman who makes for London has principally in his mind the thought of getting on in the world and getting rich. He realised that the man who addressed him was what he called back home a *dyn hysbys*, a cunning man, and he hesitated a little, "not willing to go with him among devils, from whom this magician must have derived his knowledge." Visions of wealth, position and power conjured up by the thought of these "vast treasures" soon stifled all his fears and he went down with him to Wales, taking him to the spot where he had cut the stick. Digging there under "the stock or root of a large old hazel" they came to a broad flat stone which covered the entrance to a large cavern into which they entered. Midway they came to a bell which the conjurer cautioned him on no account to touch; pushing forward again they came to a huge wide cave "and there saw many thousands of warriors lying fast asleep in a large circle, their heads outwards, every one clad in bright armour, with their swords, shields and other weapons lying by them, ready to be laid hold on in an instant whenever the bell should ring and awake them. All the arms were so highly polished and bright that they illuminated the cavern as with the light of ten thousand flames of fire. They saw amongst the warriors one greatly distinguished from the rest by his arms, shield, battle axe, and a crown of gold, set with the most precious stones, lying by his side.

"In the midst of the circle of warriors they saw two very large heaps, one of gold, the other of silver." The magician told him that he could help himself and take away from either heap as much as he could carry but not from both—the Welshman took the gold. Then he must have had a bit of a shock, for the magician refused either, adding that it was "his contempt of gold that had enabled him to acquire that superior knowledge and wisdom which he possessed."

On the way out, the Welshman, unsteady under his load of gold, was cautioned again to be careful not to touch the bell, for, if he did, one or more of the soldiers would awake and ask if it was day. "Should this happen," said the cunning man, "you must, without hesitation, answer, 'No, sleep thou on'; on which he will lay down his head and sleep." On their way up, what the magician greatly feared, happened, and the clumsy Welshman struggling with his gold touched the bell; immediately one of the warriors raised his head and asked: "Is it day?" "No," replied the Welshman, "sleep thou on." After this they got out without further mishap, replaced the stone and put back the hazel tree. Before they parted the Welshman had to listen to a brief sermon which was to the effect that with the exercise of the Christian virtues of thrift and prudence he had now enough for life, but that should some misfortune befall him he might go for more, taking care, of course, not to touch the bell. He informed him that the distinguished person was Arthur and that he and his warriors slept there "with their arms ready at hand, for the dawn of the day when the Black Eagle and the Golden Eagle should go to war, the loud clamour of which would make the earth tremble so much, that the bell would ring loudly, and the warriors awake, take up their arms and destroy all the enemies of the *Cymry*, who afterwards should repossess the island of Britain, re-establish their own working and government at

Caerlleon, and be governed with justice, and blessed with peace as long as the world endures."

Well, the Welshman, not benefiting by the "sermon," soon ran through his gold and found himself in need. Once again he visited the cave, gathered such a big sackful of gold that he failed to push through the narrow passage without touching the bell. Immediately the warriors sprang to their feet and asked if it was day, but the poor Welshman, terrified at the sight, and out of breath with his exertions, failed to give the appropriate answer, whereupon they set on him, "beat him dreadfully" and having taken the gold from him threw him out of the cave. He never recovered from the effects of this beating but remained throughout his life a cripple, and, of course, poor, because, try as he might he never again found the entrance, for the warriors, when they threw him out, "drew the stone after them over the mouth of the cave." Larded with bits of advice about the evil of covetousness and the danger of giving way to one's own wishes—except the wish to be good—the legend is made respectable for reception and circulation in the Wales of the early decades of the last century, when legends as such were taboo.

Primarily, this is a legend of hidden treasure, for the magician's first thought ran to the heaps of gold and silver that lay hidden where the stick was cut; it was only when the Welshman got his load outside that the stranger thought it worth while to say who the distinguished person was—and only then as an afterthought. The further fact that London Bridge, the starting point of the Welsh legends, figures in a widely spread English tale about buried treasure, confirms one in the conviction that they started off as buried-treasure stories.

The English story is that a certain pedlar of Swaffham, in Norfolk, dreamt that if he stood on London Bridge he would have some very good news. A shopkeeper who had noticed him loitering there went up to him on the third day and asked him what he was doing. On being told he laughed at him and said that the night before he had had a dream that he was in Swaffham, and in the dream was told that if he dug under a certain oak tree behind a pedlar's house, he would find a lot of treasure. He, however, was not so simple as to be taken in by a dream, but the pedlar was simple enough to go home and try, and there in the exact spot indicated in the shopkeeper's dream found a vast treasure.

In all these legends one is always on the look-out for hints and references that may help one to discover their antiquity. Is there any significance in the fact that the warriors were lying in a circle "with their heads outwards," for that is how the family slept in the ancient homes and halls of Wales, as described by Giraldus Cambrensis—with their feet towards the central fire-place?

A similar legend comes from Cardiganshire and is told by a noted writer and historian of that county, *Gwynionydd*. Dafydd Meirig, a farmer's son, quarrelled with his father, and like so many thousands of the men of Cardiganshire, packed his bag and went off to London. He fell in with a drover who asked him to drive a herd of cattle to London; he agreed, and to help him in that task cut a hazel stick—an extraordinary stick, for while the sticks of the other drovers were in ribbons by the time they reached London, Dafydd's was intact. On London Bridge he met a wizard who noticed his stick and told him of the treasures that lay beneath the spot where he cut it. The story now proceeds in much the same way as in the above. They returned to Wales and somewhere on this vast moor where he cut it they found the spot. They dug down and after a time came to a constructed stairway with easily manageable steps, and great lamps lighting up the whole place. In the vast underground chamber they saw, not far from the bottom of the steps, a large table near which a tall seven-foot man sat, supporting his head with his left hand, while the right—which was all red—rested on the table grasping a huge sword. Of this person, "sleeping peacefully," the wizard said that he was "*Owen Lawgoch*, who is to sleep on till some appointed time when he will awake and be the king of the Brythons. That in his hand is one of the swords of the ancient kings of Britain and no battle was lost in which that was used." They saw, besides, in every corner a vast collection of armour of the early centuries; and they somehow got to know that it was permissible for them to take a handful, but none to put in their purses, of the thousands of gold pieces bearing the images of the kings of Britain that lay on the table.

They paid other visits to the cave and on one of these Dafydd put some of the gold bearing the image of Owen's bravest ancestors in his bag—they never found the cave again!

In this version the warriors, and the bell, are missing, but their armour is there. *Owen Lawgoch* (of the red hand) has here ousted Arthur from his once secure and proud position as the hero whom Wales awaited to return to fight its battles once again and rule over its people.

King Arthur and *Owen Lawgoch* may have replaced earlier divinities that guarded these treasures, for it would seem that caves, like lakes, had guardians that kept watch over them. Was King Arthur substituted for the original divinity, only to be supplanted in his turn by *Owen Lawgoch*?

Two or three places called *Craig y Ddinas* contend for the honour of sheltering Arthur dead: one near Llantrisant and one in Ystrad Dyfodwg parish, both in Glamorgan, the other—and the one more generally favoured—a rocky eminence near Pont Neath Vaughan at the top of Neath valley, a place noted for its many and large caves. There is another claimant, *Craig y Ddinas* above the village of Llandybie, a huge mass of limestone rock in which there existed originally a cave, called *Ogof* (cave) *Cil yr Ychen*, but extensive quarrying has since eaten away the rock which formed it. Here rested, not Arthur, but *Owen Lawgoch* and his warriors. The legend is told by Howells in his *Cambrian Superstitions*: Amongst the most valiant of our leaders who fought against the Saxons was the brave chieftain, *Owen Lawgoch*, said to have been the last to sustain the conflict; in the end, however, hard pressed by his enemies, he and his gallant men "retired to a cave on the northern side of *Mynydd Mawr*, near Llandilo, Carmarthenshire, where they obtained food by foraging."

As I said at the commencement, some of these legends could equally well be placed in different categories: here there is introduced a theme which belongs to the legends of the wells, but if we are to make any sense of this legend we have to anticipate and insert it now: Having decided to make this cave their head-quarters, at least for the time being, they settled down to some kind of routine, and "every morning . . . the chief (*Owen Law-goch*) watered his horse at a fine spring . . . covered with a large stone, which required gigantic strength to lift it up; after watering his horse as usual one morning, he forgot to replace the stone, and coming there the next day was terrified at the sight of a lake of water, covering a large tract of ground where the well stood. This was occasioned by his neglecting to cover the well. After relating the circumstance to his men, they all laid themselves down in their armour, and were so overpowered with sleep that they never awoke, and *still* lie dormant in the bowels of the mountain, where, as the legend goes, they are to remain until awakened by the sound of a trumpet and the clang of arms on *Rhiwgoch*, when they will resume their pristine vigour, and issuing from the cave will conquer their Saxon enemies and drive them from their land." And so it is called *Llyn-llechwen* (or *Llechowen*).

There is a sequel to this story which has been seized upon by the local people as confirming the truth of the legend. Under a nearby hill called *Craig y Derwyddon*, quarrymen, in 1813, came across a large cave that nobody knew anything at all about—though it seems to have had a name, *Ogof Pant-y-llyn!*—in which were discovered the skeletons of very tall men. It was no wonder the men said when they found them that the old legend was true after all.

This is not all. The district of Llandybie seems to have been the centre and stronghold of the cult of *Owen Lawgoch*, for it possesses another legend which says that Owen was sent by the king to *Ystrad Towy* to unite the Welsh tribes against their enemies. It proved an unpleasant task and Owen was wounded, presumably at Dynefor Castle, for he is said to have ridden from there on his white charger as far as *Derwydd* to seek refuge, but was turned away despite the fact that his arm was bleeding and that he was so obviously in need of succour. Away he went with a sad heart, and three days later his body was found in *Cil-yr-Ychen-cave*, having bled to death. Outside the cave neighing piteously was his horse, which, on their discovering his master's body, fell dead on the spot.

No dramatic details of finding the cave and discovering treasure; no bell to ring; no awakened warriors calling "is it day?" adorn this story. No ancient sword, with magic power, is grasped and no dog or carved chair is seen—it may well be an early example of the sleeping hero legend.

King Arthur we know, but who was this mythic hero *Owen Lawgoch*? It is just possible that he was a real person—more real than Arthur—for there was an *Owen Lawgoch ap Thomas ap Rhodri ap Llywellyn Fawr*, who fought against the English in the French wars of Edward III. His brilliant campaigns on the Continent must have brought him much notoriety in his own country, and as his chosen opponents were consistently the English, it is easy to see how he and his brave band of Welshmen could slip into the position once securely held in the imagination of the people by King Arthur.

Owen escaped to France to complain to the king that Edward III had put his father to death, and had seized his possessions. Philip received him with great favour and entrusted him with many military undertakings, but his great aim was to restore, in alliance with France and Spain, the independence of Wales. In 1369 he sailed from Harfleur with a fleet supplied by Charles V, but rough weather drove him back; in 1372 he made another attempt and was to be joined in the channel by the Spanish fleet. This attempt also proved abortive. When on a later expedition he was besieging Mortagne-sur-Mer, an English spy of the name of John Lamb came to him and pretended that he had good news from his own countrymen, who were ready, he said, for his return and would rise in his support as one man—and then treacherously slew him. But his place was to be taken by another Owen (Owen Glyndwr) now only nineteen years of age. So *Owen Lawgoch* passes out of life and—who knows—into legend. For a full treatment of the identity of *Owen Lawgoch—Yeuain de Galles* —see *The Transactions of the Society of Cymmrodorion* (1901, p. 6) where Edward Owen and Sir John Rhys enter into full discussion of the whole matter.

North Wales, not to be outdone by the South, also lays claim to be the guardian of Arthur's resting place: "In the steep precipice on the left, near the upper end of *Llyn Llydaw* (in Snowdonia) there is a cave . . . called the Cave of the Youth of Eryri" (*Ogof Llanciau Yryri*). King Arthur and his young men fell in with the enemy at *Tregalan* and pushed up *Bwlch y Saethau*, where from a discharge of arrows (*saethau*) Arthur was killed and where he was "buried under a huge stone mound." Afterwards "all his men ascended the peak of *Lliwedd*, and descended thence to an immense cave in one of the steep ascents of *Cwm Dyli*. When all had entered in . . . the mouth of the cave was closed with the loose stone and turf." They all then lay down on their shields and went to sleep, there to remain till the second coming of Arthur. A shepherd of *Cwm Dyli* came across them some years ago, still there, still asleep. He was one of a party of shepherds rounding up the sheep on that part of Snowdon when one sheep fell on to a precipitous ledge. Perilous as the descent was he ventured down, and when he came there he was astonished to find the mouth of a cave, in which upon looking in he saw a light burning and an innumerable host of soldiers asleep on their shields. He pushed his way in and in doing so "knocked his head against a bell. . . . The soldiers immediately woke up and as they awoke gave forth a terrific shout. The shepherd got such a fright that he was never well again." There is no treasure in this legend, but the most remarkable thing in it is that Arthur is shown as sleeping apart from his "youths."

Another cave legend comes from North Wales which is of some interest as it purports to explain the origin of the name *Lawgoch*: A long time ago, the good people of *Nanhwynan* were sorely troubled by the depredations of an audacious robber who used to break into their houses, robbing them of food, milking the goats and the cows and taking away the best of the sheep. This went on for a long time. But one day one of the shepherds returning from the mountain saw a big burly man, covered all over with reddish hair, resting on one of the neighbouring hills. By taking a roundabout way home he managed to escape his attention—for he had a suspicion that he might be the robber.

The Hairy Man

Plans were made at once to catch him and they all set out, but immediately he caught sight of them he sprang to his feet and was soon out of sight, leaping over hill and dale like a roe. Constant watch was kept and he was again seen basking in the sun; and though they set their dogs on him he bounded away like a hare and was out of sight.

It was clear now that they had to get the help of a magician. He advised them to get a red greyhound without a single hair of any other shade in his coat. They managed to get one and when they got another glimpse of the hairy man they set it after him, but once again, leaping down a steep cliff, he escaped. He was, however, caught in the end: In a small farmhouse there lived a courageous woman who, roused by a deep resentment at her frequent losses, sat up to watch. About midnight she heard a noise outside the window, which she stealthily approached, hatchet in hand, ready for a most desperate encounter. When she got there he was half-way in through the window but when he saw her he suddenly drew back, but not before she got in a mighty blow which completely severed his right hand. Next morning the men following the spots of blood traced him to his cave under a waterfall. As he was never seen again, it was believed that he died of his injury and so the cave has ever since been known as the Cave of *Owen Lawgoch*, or the Cave of the Hairy Man.

It savours really of the legends of the giants, but is given here because it is of some interest in connexion with *Owen Lawgoch*.

One would expect the land of Gwent where, at Caerleon, King Arthur held his court, to have some legend of him, and so it proves. A Monmouthshire farmer troubled by a bogy decided to go to Caerleon to consult a wizard. On his way he met a strange-looking old man in a three-cornered hat who asked him if he would like to see "something of a wonder." Nothing loth, he went with him; by and by they came to a wood where his guide sprang from his horse and kicked aside a huge stone which instantly moved, disclosing the mouth of a large cave. Having tied their horses, they went in and down a flight of steps, until they came to a vast chamber where they saw "hundreds of men lying full length on the floor; each with his head reposing on the stock of his gun." The farmer was told that these were "Arthur's thousand soldiers . . . sleeping till the *Kymry* have need of them." On their way out the farmer accidentally touched one of the two bells which the stranger had specially warned him against. The whole host rose to their feet and shouted, "Are the *Kymry* in straits?" "Not yet," replied the man in the three-cornered hat, "sleep thou on," whereupon they all dropped down again on their guns. Before they parted the old man warned him "on pain of death not to utter a syllable about what you have seen for the space of a year and a day: if you do so woe awaits you." The farmer never saw him again nor was he able to find the mouth of the cave.*

* For an extensive treatment of the undying hero legend and King Arthur, see the opening chapters of Christina Hole's *English Folk-heroes.*

Chapter Nine

LEGENDS OF THE WELLS

WELLS played quite a big part in the life and imagination of the Welsh people in Christian as well as in pre-Christian times. The cult of the wells was so deeply rooted in the life of the people that not even the Christian Church was able to eradicate it. The many sacred wells endowed with healing powers to be found up and down the country, dedicated to the patron saints of the parishes, and made the objects of pilgrimages, amount to a confession of its failure. Sir John Rhys in his *Hibbert Lectures* 1886, on *The Growth of Religion as illustrated by Celtic Heathendom*, says : "It is curious to observe that, while Christian missionaries appear to have made comparatively short work of the greater Celtic gods of Aryan origin, the Church fulminated in vain against the humble worship of wells and stocks and stones. The cult required no well-defined and costly priesthood which could be overturned once for all, and, a little modified, it thrives in some Celtic lands to this day. All that the Church could do was to ignore it for a time, and ultimately to assimilate it : to effect its annihilation has always been beyond her power." The legends vary considerably in their character and motifs and are difficult to define: holy wells invariably became healing wells; some became again mere wishing wells, or oracular wells; indeed, they may have been such before they ever became "holy" wells.

One theme in quite a number is that of the negligent user or guardian who fails to put the covering stone back, with the result that a whole town or a large area is inundated. We have already given one in connexion with *Owen Lawgoch.*

It has, however, a variant which tells how a well on Mynydd Mawr became a lake—*Llyn Llech Owen*: A man by the name of Owen lived at *Dyllgoed Uchaf*, on whose land the well was situated. Every day he took his horse to water to this well and was always most careful to replace the flat stone which formed its cover. It unfortunately happened that one day he forgot and was riding home leisurely when he casually looked back, and lo and behold! the waters had already overflowed a large area. He swung back and galloped round the water as fast as he could; thus only was he able to arrest the flow of water, for it would not overrun the track left by the horse. It has ever since been called after him—the Lake of Owen's Flag-stone (*Llyn Llech Owen*).

Similar legends profess to tell how many of our lakes were formed, amongst them *Llyn Tegid*, or Bala Lake, which owes its origin to the negligence of some person to replace the stone on *Ffynnon Gywer* (Gywer's Well) which at that time was in the centre of the old town. In the morning both town and district had been inundated and a sheet of water three miles long and one wide covered the whole area.

Such, too, is the legend of *Ffynnon Grassi* (Grace's Well) in the parish of Llangybi. It had a cover which had always to be kept on, except when the well was being used, or else its water would burst forth and drown the whole place. Through somebody's neglect this did happen, and the nearby *Glasfryn* Lake was formed, at the corner of which the well may still be seen. Grassi—probably a modern substitution for the older and forgotten name—is supposed to have been the owner, or at least the person who failed to replace the stone, and to have been so overcome with remorse that when she saw the disastrous waters she wandered up and down "moaning and weeping." Indeed, she is still heard at times in the vicinity of the lake, bewailing her negligence. She also paid visits to the nearby house, making herself such a nuisance that it became difficult to keep servants. She is described as "a tall lady with well marked features and large bright eyes . . . dressed in white silk and a white velvet bonnet." Near the lake is a field called *Cae'r Ladi*, (The Lady's Field) in which she has been seen and in which there is an ancient standing stone resembling the figure of a hurrying female. At one time this stone was white-washed (presumably by the family), adorned with a bonnet and draped over the "shoulders" with a shawl. I wonder if these little attentions sprang from the suspicion that the stone might bear some relationship to, indeed, might be the petrified figure, of the person whose negligence caused the well to overflow, for the lamenting wail was often heard to come from that direction. It would not be an impossible thought to people familiar with the fate of Lot's wife.

This Grassi, in what appears to be another story, is said to have been seized by the fairies for her criminal negligence and turned into a swan. In that form she continued to live for sixty years, and then died, loudly lamenting her lot.

To this class—stories of overflowing wells—belongs that of the drowning of the Lower Hundred (*Cantre'r Gwaelod*). It differs from the others only in being on a very much larger scale and consequently more disastrous in its effects. The first version we have of it may be found in the Black Book of Carmarthen where the blame is put on a damsel. Subsequent story-tellers have intro-duced great dykes with towers and gates and sluices, and put a drunken prince in charge—attractive, nay irresistible material for later exploitation in Wales. Thus it ceased to be a simple legend of the wells and grew into a lake legend akin to those in which a wicked prince brings down upon himself and his household the vengeance of God; so *Seithenyn*, the drunkard, is involved in the disastrous inundation that follows upon his criminal negligence.

This rich lowland stretch, forming the lordship of *Gwyddno Garanhir* (the long-legged), lay out under what is now Cardigan Bay. As it was below the level of the sea it was protected by a great dyke the gates of which were opened when the tide was going out, to allow the waters of the rivers to flow through, and closed again when the tide was coming in. The custodianship of this embankment was considered an office of great honour and the person who filled it at this time was *Seithenyn* the son of *Seithyn Seidi*, king of *Dyfed*. He is referred to in the Triads as one of three arrant drunkards of the Isle of Britain. According to the same Triads this lowland hundred possessed sixteen of the finest cities in Wales with the exception only of Caerleon-on-Usk. Great banquets were held from time to time in the courts of *Gwyddno* and *Seithenyn* and it was at one of these, when the revelry was at its highest, that disaster overtook them. As was customary in a Welsh banquet a harpist was present to entertain the guests and lead in the chorus—perhaps one in praise of the blue buffalo horn:

> Fill high the blue horn, the blue buffalo horn;
> Fill high the long silver-rimmed buffalo horn:
> While the roof of the hall by our chorus is torn,
> Fill, fill to the brim the deep silver-rimmed horn.

It was the harpist who first discovered that doom was upon them, and he warned them to flee for their lives, but *Gwyddno* tried to calm them: there was no reason to fear, was not *Seithenyn* at the gates? When he looked round *Seithenyn* was helplessly drunk and utterly oblivious of the peril that threatened them all. Panic broke out: they rushed for the doors; outside, above the sound of the storm they heard shrieks of terror and cries of lamentation. Soon all was quiet, the sea had silenced them for ever. *Gwyddno*, his court, a number of followers and the harpist —a favoured person in all these legends—escaped and made for the high grounds of Lleyn and Snowdonia, "places uninhabited before."

That in brief is the legend. As I said, it had obvious attractions for the story-teller and Thomas Love Peacock in his *The Misfortunes of Elphin* has exploited to the full its dramatic possibilities. When day broke *Gwyddno* looked out and surveyed the disaster: he said not a word, but he uttered a sigh, the echo of which, in the form of a proverb, has come down to this day:

> Ochenaid Gwyddno Garanhir
> Pan droes y don dros ei dir.
> The sigh of Gwyddno Garanhir
> When the wave rolled over his land.

There is preserved in the *Myvyrian Archaiology* (I, 165) a short poem attributed to Gwyddno where he pronounces maledictions upon the head of *Seithenyn* and calls upon him to listen to the cries of the perishing and to view the effects of his drunkenness:

"Stand forward Seithenyn and behold the dwelling of heroes—the plain of Gwyddno the ocean covers!

Accursed be the sea guard, who after his carousal let loose the destroying fountain of the raging deep.

Accursed be the watcher, who after his drunken revelry, loosed the fountain of the desolating sea.

A cry from the sea arises above the ramparts; even to heaven does it ascend—after the fierce excess comes the long cessation!

A cry from the sea ascends above the ramparts; even to heaven does the supplication come!—after the excess there ensues restraint!

A cry from the sea awakens me this night!—

A cry from the sea arises above the winds!

A cry from the sea impels me from my place of rest this night!

After excess comes the far extending death!"

From being an opulent prince *Gwyddno* was reduced to maintaining himself on the produce of one fishing weir, near his home, "on the strand between the Dyfi and Aberystwyth." Nevertheless it was a most valuable fishery, and every May eve the value of £100 was taken from it. He possessed also a marvellous basket, regarded as one of the thirteen precious things of the Isle of Britain: if there was put into it the food for just one man, when it was opened, there would be found in it enough for a hundred men.

Another lowland district in North Wales between Beaumaris and Penmaen Mawr, the possession of Prince Helyg, was lost in much the same way, being submerged while the prince and his

friends were banqueting. Again the harpist is the first to discover
the disaster, and escapes.

A large tract must have been devoured above Abergele, for on
a gravestone in the churchyard is the following epitaph:

> Here lies, in the churchyard of St. Michael's,
> A man whose dwelling was five miles to the North!

To return to the wells. There were holy wells in every parish,
dedicated to the patron saint, of which some, like that of St.
Winefred in North Wales, acquired island-wide fame. We had
two in my native parish, and that of St. Celer became very
famous, drawing pilgrims well into the eighteenth century. The
reader will pardon me for choosing as an example the holy well
of St. Celer, the patron saint of my native parish, for the scenes
enacted here were repeated in the case of the majority of them.

There were also in the parish medicinal wells, or springs, which
were resorted to by large numbers well into this century. Folk
had long ceased to bathe in the well of St. Celer; the transfer of
affection from one well to the other taking place gradually, the
vogue of the medicinal increasing in proportion to the decay of
the medieval superstition.

The scene at St. Celer's well is described by Edward Llwyd in
his *Parochialia*: "Not far from the church at the bottom of a steep
hill issueth a fountain. Over the fall thereof a little chapel is
erected. Hither every summer infirm people make a frequent
resort, but particularly from the 21st of June to the feast of St.
Peter (29th) there will be such a concourse of people that no fair
in Wales can equal it in multitude, out of an opinion that the
saint endued it with such a virtue as will cure all infirmities.
The tradition obtains that about two years since, some infirm
persons left their crutches behind in the church in memory of
their being cured by bathing in this well. But I doubt there was
in this much of the monkish *piae fraudes*. However, there are
persons alive this day that saw the crutches. In the churchyard
there is a place which I may properly call a cemetery (in Welsh
it is called *Lhech* (*llech*)) where after bathing, the infirm must lie
down to sleep, which as many do are persuaded will recover,

otherwise not." The *Llech*, or slab, lay probably over the saint's grave near the north door of the old church. Not all this crowd, "that no fair in Wales can equal," were there to seek healing; they were there to see miracles, to see crutches thrown sky-high, to hear ejaculations of gratitude, to mix with their friends and to have a holiday.

Much more famous, of course, was *Ffynnon Gwenfrewi* (St. Winefred's Well) in Holywell, and much more magnificent the chapel built over it. It could boast of papal privileges and royal visitors and benefactors. Undoubtedly the cruel and barbaric act which led to its miraculous origin helped to fix it vividly and permanently on the imagination of the people and to surround it with a unique sacredness:

Gwenfrewi, a virtuous maiden, the daughter of a local chief, lived in the seventh century. Caradog, a neighbouring prince, fell violently in love with her beauty, but she refused his advances and ran away. The rejected youth followed her and in his rage drew his sword and cut off her head. It rolled down the hill, and where it came to rest, there gushed forth a spring of healing water. St. Beuno, her mother's brother, took up the head and fixing it to the body, miraculously restored her to life again, none the worse for her decapitation save that a thin white ring marked the place where he joined it to the body. *Gwenfrewi* lived for another fifteen years, and, dying as abbess of *Gwytherin* in Denbighshire, was buried there. (See *Lives of the Saints*, under St. Beuno and St. Winefred. See also Thomas Pennant's *Tours in Wales*, Vol. I, p. 40, for a description of the well at the end of the eighteenth century.)

There was one very famous well in north Pembrokeshire, under the shadow of the Prescelly Mountains—St. Teilo's Well. The church—*Llandeilo Llwydiarth*—now in ruins, stood near Maenclochog and in a field about 200 yards from *Llandeilo* Farm. The well healed a wide range of ailments including whooping cough, but virtue was not only in the well, but also in the holy relic used in drinking its waters, nothing less than the skull of the saint himself. The story is told that this illustrious saint, bracketed with *Cadog* and *Dewi* in eminence, a founder of many churches and a Bishop of Llandaff, had a favourite maid, a native of this parish. On his death-bed he charged her to take, a twelvemonth from the day of his burial, his skull from Llandeilo Fawr in Carmarthenshire and bring it to his church in Pembrokeshire, so that all who ailed might be restored by drinking the water of the well out of it.

The skull had been in the possession of the family at the farm for hundreds of years—a family by the unusual name of *Melchior* (pronounced Melshor), but of Cymric stock and tongue. Mr. Melchior considered himself the hereditary guardian of this relic. It was part of the ritual that the water should be handed in the skull to the patient by a member of the family, and by nobody else—some said the heir should perform this office. However, it was believed that it should be somebody born in the house. This may point to the proprietary rights of the medieval priest; the condition safeguarding his sole right to the use of the skull, and, therefore, to any gift that might be customary.

The Melchiors charged nothing for their service, nor did they believe in the efficacy of the skull or the well, still they obliged all who came—and many came within living memory. A man brought his son all the way from Glamorgan, but returned none the better for the long journey. Then they remembered that the water had not been drunk out of the skull, so they came back, repaired their previous neglect, with the result that the son was completely restored.

Very serious doubts have been entertained as to the genuineness of this relic; for it is the skull, according to Baring Gould, who examined it, of a young person, and "seems almost certain to have been . . . a young woman's!" But all has now gone. The skull, *Penglog Teilo*, was sold for £50 by Miss Melchior, the last of the family, to a person who represented himself as acting on behalf of some museum or other, and so she was induced to part with it. Nobody now knows of its whereabouts. Belief in its efficacy had, however, waned and no sick came any more; the well itself—as a sacred well—has gone, too, for a ram has been erected in it, as I am informed in a letter from the present Vicar of Maenclochog, the Reverend T. Hamer, to carry water to a

Washing in well

nearby dwelling-house. It is enough to make poor Teilo turn in his three graves—and thereby hangs another tale:

When the saint died three churches contended for his body, Penalun, in Pembrokeshire, where he was born, Llandeilo Fawr in Carmarthenshire, and the cathedral church of Llandaff of which he was once bishop. As they could not agree it was decided to have "recourse to fasting and prayer." In the morning they beheld three bodies of the saint and all exactly the same, so each church was satisfied, and St. Teilo had three graves. The possession of the body—which meant relics—of a saintly person of great eminence and holiness was a great advantage to a church in the Middle Ages, for it enhanced its ecclesiastical status and, as a centre of pilgrimages, brought it great financial gain.

At the holy well of St. Tegla, near the parish church of Llandegla in Denbighshire, a very curious ritual was observed. The water was said to be under the tutelage of the saint and to be specially efficacious in the cure of *Clwyf Tegla*, epilepsy, or fits. "In order to inspire the votaries with greater awe," the sick person was not to begin operations before sunset; he then proceeded to the well, washed his limbs in it, threw in an offering of four pence, and then walked round the well three times, each time repeating the Lord's Prayer. After this he went into the churchyard and walked round the church three times, again repeating each time the Lord's Prayer.

I should have said that in all these movements the votary carried with him in a basket a fowl—if a man, a cock, if a woman, a hen. It accompanied him also into church, where he spent the night, sleeping under the altar with the Bible under his head and covered with a cloth or a carpet. In the morning he got up, made an offering of sixpence, released the bird in church and went home. If the bird died he would recover, for the disease was then supposed to have passed to it. As late as 1855 old people remembered seeing the "birds staggering about from the effects of the fits which had been transferred to them."

Lying down on the gravestone or tomb of the saint was a fairly general practice. Here the altar may have been built over Tegla's grave, or her relics may have been buried there.

A well that had acquired more than local notoriety was *Ffynnon Eilian*, in the parish of Llandrillo yn Rhos, Denbighshire. From having once been a holy and a healing well, it turned over to another kind of business and became a cursing well (*Ffynnon reibio*). This was a shrewd move by someone who realised that there was a need and a demand for such a service. In an unregenerate world where wrongs are committed and injustices flourish, a well of this kind was a great boon. Not many dared to stand up to a grabbing landlord, for fear of the consequences; how much easier was it to go, long after dark, to the keeper of the well of Eilian, to set in motion its imprecatory powers, and then for the next few weeks to have the secret pleasure of seeing the oppressor gradually pining away until he eventually, like all the wicked, perished.

It filled the place of the conjurer also in that it could be "the instrument of discovering thieves and of recovering stolen goods" after, of course, first invoking the aid of the saint by prayer in the nearby church.

The procedure—in the business of cursing—was in this wise, and is described in Lewis's *Topographical Dictionary of Wales*, under *Llandrillo yn Rhôs*: "Even in this present age [this noted well] is annually visited by some hundreds of people, for the reprehensible purpose of invoking curses upon the heads of those who have grievously offended them. The ceremony is performed by the applicant standing upon a certain spot near the well, whilst the owner of it reads passages of the sacred scriptures, and then, taking a small quantity of water, gives it to the former to drink, and throws the residue over his head, which is repeated three times, the party continuing to mutter his imprecations in whatever terms his vengeance may dictate."

Another writer gives an entirely different form of procedure—it is possible that successive keepers did not observe the same ritual. A gift was made to the owner, or keeper, of the well, who then wrote down the name of the person to be put under a curse on a piece of paper, stuck a pin into it and then threw it into the well. It would seem that some moderation was used and a limit observed in the curses called down upon one's enemies. Death no doubt was desired by those who were accustomed to be swayed violently by likes and dislikes, others went no further than to call for pains and aches in the body, or material misfortunes such as the loss of farm stock.

The well would seem to work in this way: The enemy or victim was in some way considered to be sufficiently identified with or represented by the inscribed paper for him to be affected immediately the well got it into itself. By some sympathetic magic the well began to operate once it had the person's name in its possession. Instead of a piece of paper, a pebble inscribed with the initials, together with a pin, was sometimes thrown in, while the name was entered on a register. Pennant himself while on his tours was threatened with the vengeance of St. Eilian by a person who imagined he had been injured by him.

When a person discovered that his name was in the well, or, perhaps, with the oncoming of aches and pains in his limbs and losses amongst his cattle, began to suspect it, he would go to the guardian of the well and ask if his name had been put into it. If that was so, and the guardian agreeable, which he no doubt could be rendered by a suitable gift, the curse could be removed by erasing his name from the register and taking the inscribed pebble or bit of paper out of the well. It would no longer have any power over him. There was nothing to prevent the original person when he failed to notice any misfortune befalling his enemy from going again to the well to cancel the removal by a larger gift. The office of keeper was truly a lucrative one.

What was the significance and character of the office or position held by these persons, variably referred to as "keepers," "owners" or "guardians," were they in the succession of the original priest or divinity of the well?

There is no suggestion that anyone could go direct to the well of St. Eilian and personally invoke its aid; the request had to go to the keeper, or owner, who alone seems to have possessed the true succession and the valid *orders* to perform this service. In the case of the Melchior family the evidence would seem to be stronger. "In this particular instance we have a succession which seems to point unmistakably to an ancient priesthood of a sacred spring"—sacred probably before the time of St. Teilo and, possibly, one of the reasons "why the site was chosen by a Christian missionary."

Holy wells were naturally healing wells, most of which declined in time into mere wishing wells or oracular wells, where men sought omens, and the identity of those who had robbed them or were secretly injuring them, and assurances about the constancy and loyalty of their lovers.

In the case of St. Mary's well in the parish of Llanbedrog, in Lleyn, it was necessary that the devotee should first of all kneel before it and avow his faith in it. If a person wished to discover, for example, who had robbed him, he dropped a piece of bread in the well and named the man he suspected; if the bread sank at the mention of his name, he, right enough, was the thief. Sometimes he was wrong in his suspicions—that is, according to the piece of bread—he then had to go through all the names he could think of until the bread sank; the person named as it did so was the thief. It was resorted to also for its curative virtues in a wide range of human and animal ailments.

When young people in the neighbourhood of *Ffynnon Saethon*, in Caernarvonshire, wished to find out whether their lovers were sincere and loyal, they visited the well and threw pins into it. If the pin floated, all was well, if not there was room for doubt. These pins were presumably spikes of the blackthorn, which were often used by farmers to fasten sacks on their backs in wet weather.

Ffynnon Gwynedd, in the parish of Abererch, was the resort of those who wished to find out whether a sick person would recover or die from the complaint that afflicted him: A garment of his was thrown into the water and all they had to do was to watch to which side it drifted before it sank.

Girls, again, to discover whether their lovers were sincere, spread their handkerchiefs on the water of the well of Cybi (Llangybi); if they were pushed to the south all was well, if to the north, the contrary.

It was believed that the partner who drank first out of St.

Keynan's well (Llangurig) and Cynon's well (Llangynwyd) after the marriage ceremony became inevitably the master.

Many of these wells continued, besides, to be resorted to for the cure of various ailments, and it was believed in North Wales that a healing well had to have its flow towards the south.

Cybi's well possessed at one time what was regarded as a sacred eel, which, to the great "concern" of the villagers, was taken out. They believed that this greatly reduced the powers of the well; bathers in search of health considered it a good sign to see it coiling itself about their legs!

Ffynnon Beris (Llanberis) possessed two sacred fishes. If one of them showed itself while the sick bathed it was a good omen; if neither appeared there was no cure.

North Welsh writers have been most assiduous in collecting their folk-lore, and the reader will note that the majority of the wells referred to in this chapter are associated with that part of the country, but a large number, too, pertaining to South Wales may be found in J. Ceredig Davies's *Welsh Folklore*.

In the churchyard of St. Edren's, midway between Fishguard and Haverfordwest, there was a well noted for its cure of hydrophobia. Once, a woman was wicked enough to wash clothes in it on Sunday, with the result that the well dried up. The healing virtues, however, were transferred to the grass around, which people took home and ate with their food with equally good results. A similar sacrilege was perpetrated by a woman in a well in Co. Cork, with the result that that well dried up too.

It was the custom to dip sick infants in the well of St. Beuno, then take them into the church and lay them on a bed of rushes in the font throughout the night.

The reader may be familiar with the sight of a rag well. The fundamental ideas behind the practice reveal the simplicity and directness of the peasant mind, and are easily understandable. It is never wise to attribute profound notions and abstruse theories to peasant folk; the most natural theory that will account for the majority of the practices is most likely to be the correct one, though some must remain obscure. The practice prevailed in South Wales as well as in North Wales, but North Welsh writers seem to have recorded more numerous instances and with more interesting details.

To return to *Ffynnon Eilian*, the rag-covered bushes around testified that it had not only cursing powers but curative properties as well. If one looked more carefully at the rags one would find that they were tied to the branches with unspun wool, that is with raw wool as one gets it from the back of the sheep.

It was believed that a person on his way to a well to get rid of warts had to pick up wool which the sheep had dropped, prick each wart with a pin, rub the wart with this wool, and after throwing a bent pin into the well, place the wool on the first whitethorn bush he saw on the way back—as the wind scattered the wool so were the warts "scattered." But what is of interest here is that it had to be raw wool.

At the well of *Cefn Lleithfan* in Lleyn one had, in going to, and coming from, the well, not to say a word to anybody, nor turn to look back. Would not this be the natural desire of anyone who wished to concentrate alone on his recovery? The warts were bathed with greasy rags which were then carefully hidden under a stone at the mouth of the well. This practice, too, was known elsewhere. But as a rule the rag or bandage that had been in touch with the affected part was hung on the branches of a nearby tree or on a bush, and as the wind and the rain broke up and wore away the rag so would the ailment vanish with its disappearance. This course was not always followed. Sometimes the rag was first dipped in the well, and the affected parts bathed with it before it was tied to a branch. It was natural for the peasant, by a simple process of reasoning, to believe that a rag or a bandage which had been in close contact with the disease would absorb it, and that in leaving it on the branches he was leaving the disease there as well. Invariably, a pin, a button, or something else made of metal, was dropped into the well as a gift, or offering, to the presiding spirit or divinity.

Chapter Ten

LEGENDS OF ANIMALS
AND BIRDS

IN the legend of the Stray Cow, *Y Fuwch Gyfeiliorn*, we are
back again in the world of the lake-fairies, for this famous cow
belonged to the ladies of *Llyn Barfog*, an upland lake not far
from Aberdovey. These ladies, dressed in green, were in the habit
of making their appearance in the evenings in the vicinity of the
lake, accompanied by their milk-white hounds. They possessed,
too, a herd of milk-white cows, which grazed around the lake
and were a familiar sight to the people of the neighbourhood.
One day a farmer was lucky enough to catch one of them, which
had presumably strayed to his own herd. Never was a farmer
more fortunate, for there was never such another cow, never such
calves, such milk, such butter and such cheese. The fame of this
wonderful cow spread throughout the whole district, and the
farmer, from being a poor man, became rich, and the owner of a
vast herd. With the increase of wealth there came an increase of
pride and greed, and when he realised that the cow was getting
old and would cease to be of any value to him, he determined to

133

get all the profit he could out of her, so he began to fatten her for the butcher. Here again she proved an extraordinary cow and fattened so easily and quickly that she became almost a monstrosity of fatness. The killing day came, the neighbours gathered together to see the sight, the butcher arrived with the necessary tackle and the farmer had every reason to be pleased with the cow, the crowd and the prospects. Everything was at last ready for the butcher to strike the blow that would stun and fell the cow. His hand was already in the air when something happened! A piercing cry "that awakened an echo in a dozen hills" was heard, the axe fell from the butcher's paralysed hand, and when the crowds looked in the direction from which the cry came they saw one of the ladies of the lake, clad in green, standing on a prominent crag above the waters of *Llyn Barfog*, calling, with uplifted arms, and in accents loud as thunder, her stray cow home:

"*Dere di Velen Einion,*
    Cyrn Cyfeiliorn—braith y Llyn,
 	
A'r voel Dodin,
Codwch, dewch adre."
	"Come thou, Einion, yellow one,
	    Stray horns—speckled one of the
	        Lake,
	    And the hornless Dodin,
	    Arise, come home."

Immediately this voice was heard the fairy cow with her progeny, to the third and fourth generation, ran towards the lake. Momentarily stunned by what had happened the farmer soon recovered and set off after them as hard as he could, but he caught none of them, he merely witnessed the final scene on the lake as the lady in green, surrounded by the famous cow and her progeny, disappeared beneath the waters, waving her hands as she did so. The cows, tossing their heads, followed her. On the spot where each vanished there appeared a yellow water-lily. The farmer had time enough to rue the sad consequences of his greed, for the prosperity which the stray cow brought departed with her, and he was reduced to greater poverty than before.

Another legend, not to be confused with the above, bearing the title *Y Fuwch Laethwen Lefrith*—the Milk-white Milch Cow—is given in the *Iolo MSS.* "The milk-white cow gave enough of milk to every one who desired it; and however frequently milked, or by whatever number of persons, she was never found deficient. All persons who drank of her milk were healed of every illness; from being fools they became wise, and from being wicked, became happy. This cow went round the world, and wherever she appeared, she filled with milk all the vessels that could be found; leaving calves behind her for all the wise and happy. It was from her that all the milch cows in the world were obtained. After traversing the Island of Britain, for the benefit and blessing of country and kindred, she reached the Vale of Towy; where, tempted by her fine appearance and superior condition, the natives sought to kill and eat her; but just as they were proceeding to effect their purpose, she vanished from between their hands, and was never seen again."

A house in the locality still bears the name: *Y Fuwch Laethwen Lefrith*.

A somewhat similar legend is told of another wonderful cow. She is called "The Freckled Cow" (*Y Fuwch Frech*) and had her pastureland on a hill near an upland farm called *Cefn Bannog* in the neighbourhood of Ruthin. Whenever anyone went to her for milk, she gave it generously, filling the vessel, however big it was, with milk of the richest quality, and she never became dry. This went on for a long time, until a wicked hag, envious of the people's good fortune, took a riddle and milked her dry. Immediately she vanished and was never seen again. She is said to be the mother of the two *Ychen Bannog*—the long-horned oxen which drew the *afanc* out of the lake.

With slight variations the story is known also beyond Offa's Dyke: In Shropshire she is *The White Cow of Mitchells Fold*; in other parts of England she is known as *The Dun Cow*.

Mention of the two *Ychen Bannog* reminds one of another legend connected with them. They were used to haul stone for the building of the church of St. David at Llanddewi Brefi, but the ground was so rough and the way so steep that one of the poor beasts exerted himself to such an extent that he dropped down dead, whereupon the other bellowed nine times with such force that the hill in front of him split in half and he was able to drag the load along with perfect ease. This rhyme has ever since been connected with the place:

Llanddewi Brefi fraith,	Llanddewi Brefi the spotted
Lle brefodd yr ych naw gwaith.	Where the ox bellowed nine times.

According to Meyrick, the county historian, there used to be preserved in this church the "inside of a large petrified horn about a foot long and very porous," measuring at the base 17 inches in circumference. Professor Boyd Dawkins has declared that it belonged to the great urus, *Bos Primigenius*, such as "Charlemagne hunted in the forest of Aachen." This relic has now found its way to a private residence. The base measurements of the horn—17 inches—may help one to visualise the enormous size of the pair that adorned the head of each ox.

A large number of animals figure in the Lives of the Welsh saints. These are the *true legends*: *legenda*, things to be read. They, that is, the Lives, were read during the time of divine service on the festivals of the particular saints, with the purpose of inciting the people to a greater piety and to an emulation of their deeds and sacrifices.

A rather curious one tells how a little mouse helped St. Cadog and his disciples: After returning from Ireland, with many Irish clergy, he had a desire to improve his Latin "after the Roman manner," and for that purpose withdrew into Breconshire, where he had heard a "celebrated Italian rhetorician" had settled. The Italian was quite prepared to accept him and his disciples, but as there was a severe famine in the land he doubted whether he would be able to feed them. Cadog immediately called upon the help of God, "wherefore on that very day it happened that a mouse, having come out of its hole, bore quickly in its mouth to the blessed Cadog a grain of corn, and playfully placed it under his eyes on a writing tablet set before him. The same mouse, going and returning seven times, carried . . . as many grains of wheat. So he (Cadog) gathered those grains and hid them in his writing-roll, apprehending by this token that the divine compassion was nigh to him." He then sent for the rhetorician to tell him of what had happened and to tell him too, I think, of what they

136

were about to find. Catching the little mouse, he asks a certain widow for a length of long, fine thread. "This being tied to the foot of the mouse, he follows it as it proceeds with the thread relaxed, until (it) arrives at a certain tumulus under which there was a very beautiful subterranean house, built of old, and filled with clean wheat. And there having soon slipped through a dark hole within, and having quickly returned, it carried back in its mouth one grain, as before, of corn." This store they shared with all the poor people of the place, and his grandfather, Brychan, gave him for his monastery that part of the field where the tumulus was.

St. Illtud was much troubled by flocks of birds which were devouring his ripe corn, so he put his scholars in the fields to guard it, arming each one with a sling. Now Samson proved an utter failure at this work and was greatly worried because the swarms paid no heed to his efforts at all. He thought about it and he prayed about it and then "it was given to him from heaven to drive the birds from the corn without their flying." They tried to fly, but they utterly failed, so Samson drove them in front of him like a flock of geese; when they arrived at the barn, where he intended to confine them, they entered exactly like horses or sheep, one after the other. How long they were confined in this prison is not told, but it was long enough to produce in them a very genuine and sincere repentance, which so affected Samson that he released them all again. What I fancy weighed with them more than their sorrow for their wrong-doing, was the indignity they had suffered—the birds of the air—in being driven in front of a young scholar like a flock of geese!

We have many similar stories in Welsh folk-lore, but as a rule it is the devil, in order to enable one of his favourites to get away for the day, that collects the birds and shuts them up in the barn; he himself, in the form of a big black crow, keeping guard by the door.

A British general of the name of Ligessawc, surnamed *Llaw Hir* (the long hand), had slain three of Arthur's soldiers. This angered Arthur terribly and he pursued him everywhere until he eventually sought refuge with Cadog. Everybody else was afraid to shelter him because they dreaded Arthur's revenge. After seven years with Cadog, in perfect safety, somebody betrayed him to Arthur, who came to the river Usk with a large force and demanded his surrender. The saint asked him if he would submit the matter to the verdict of eminent judges, and as Arthur consented, five of the senior judges of all Britain, with many clergy, were summoned to the banks of the Usk. Each party took up its stand on its own side of the river. They argued for a long time: some thought that Arthur should be given three cows for each soldier, others that he should have a hundred, and that view prevailed. Arthur plays a very churlish part in the whole transaction: first of all he would not have cows of all one colour, they had to be red in the fore part and white in the hind part. It looked as if Arthur was trying to be as awkward as he could; nobody had ever heard of such cows nor knew where they could be found. However, Cadog came to the rescue and ordered some young men in the company to get him a hundred heifers of any colour; when they came he changed them to the colour required.

The next question was how to get them to Arthur, for the Usk flowed between them; after some deliberation the judges directed that Cadog's men should drive them as far as the middle of the river and that Arthur and his men should be responsible for them from there on. Anxious to get them quickly to their own side, some of Arthur's men began pulling them by the horns, when lo, and behold! they became bundles of hay in their hands.

To St. Brynach there had been given some mysterious power over wild animals. When he wished to have his furniture moved from place to place, he merely called two stags from the woods, hitched them to the wagon and drove along. After the job was done, back they went to their own once more.

The horse, though a popular animal in Wales, has not gathered round him the legends one would have expected. Vivid descriptions are given of the fleetness and prowess of the horses that figure in the *Mabinogion* and of the caparisoned steeds of King Arthur and his knights of the Round Table. There were—and still are—many sagas of the achievements of local horses on the way to the lime-kilns, and they are probably told to this day, in cracked voices by "grey old men in the corners," but they have not found their way into print.

I should like to have heard in detail that story that must have been told many a time on the lonely hearths along the *Chubut Valley* and on the *pampas* of Patagonia, where a colony of Welsh immigrants settled in the sixties of last century: Three young men under a brave and experienced settler, J. D. Evans, went out to explore the country farther west and to prospect for gold. They followed the course of the *Chubut* to a point where the tributaries *Teca* and *Lipa* fall into it; here they met a native trader who informed them of the nasty mood the natives were in, having been hunted and harassed by a column of Argentine soldiers. They at once decided to return, and rode day and night, keeping clear of the beaten paths so that they could not be followed, and arrived at the sheltered valley of *Kel-kein*. The day was wild and boisterous, when suddenly they heard the piercing war-cry of a band of natives and saw them charging madly towards them. Evans's horse *Malacara* was still fresh and in good heart, and when he heard the war-cry and felt the point of a spear in his flank, he sprang towards a deep and wide gully (*ffôs*) which he took at one leap—*a naid ofnadwy oedd honno*—and it was a terrible jump, that was! It gave Evans, however, a welcome start, and there was nothing for it now but to make for home, a hundred miles away, a journey which horse and rider did without rest or a bite to eat. I should like to have ridden that horse, but not to make that jump! Armed reinforcements from the colony returned immediately to the spot, but only to see their friends' mutilated bodies which they collected together and buried, using the Welsh Prayerbook, and singing a resurrection hymn from the old country: "*Bydd myrdd o ryfeddodau.*" See also Tschiffely: *This Way Southward.*

Evans's horse lived until it was thirty-four years of age, and lies buried in a shady corner in his garden. There, on a rock behind its grave has been carved in Spanish the following tribute of gratitude and admiration: "Here lie the remains of my horse, Whiteblaze, (Malacara) who saved my life during the attack of the Indians in the Valley of the Martyrs, on the 4th of March, 1884, as I was returning from the Cordillera."

It was unlucky to see a white horse, and old people made the sign of the cross on the back of their shoe to keep off any ill-luck until they met another white horse. If one looked at the horse after making the sign the charm was lost.

White socks were suspect and folk had a verse to warn them when about to buy a horse:

Un droed wen y ceffyl pryn,	One white sock and you may buy,
Dwy droed wen y ceffyl pryn;	Two white socks and you may still buy,
Tair droed wen, yn graff edrych arno,	Three white socks do have a care,
A phedair droed wen, dos ymaith hebddo.	Four white socks, better leave him there.

But the horses that I should like to possess were those which belonged to Cadog the Wise: they were economic to keep and involved no labour in feeding or grooming—just a coat of paint occasionally—for they were *wooden* horses! Extraordinarily swift-footed, far beyond the powers of any ordinary horse, they could make the journey from Llancarfan (near Cardiff) to Neath and Brecon and return the same day, a round journey of over a hundred and fifty miles! His servants used nothing else to bring whatever was needed from any part of the country.

A very spirited story is told by Walter Map: *Genillyn* (Cheues-lin) "of North Wales, wearing a bridle on his neck and spurs at his belt, asked shelter in South Wales at the house of Traer; and when after a sober and frugal supper they had sat long silent, he said to Traer: 'You are all wondering, yet out of respect for our customs no one asks who or whence I am. But as you are all eager to know it, I am from the north part of Wales and have been attracted to the southern parts by the renown of a noble mare which a man who lives on our and your marches keeps with such care that for a whole month past all my ambushes have been frustrated, all my attempts defeated, though . . . I have kept these tokens of bit and bridle hid.' Traer laughed . . . 'It is certainly with right and reason that your people are called cowardly and slow by ours. Any one of us would sooner for honour's sake have been caught in a valiant . . . attempt at theft, and have died a hard death, than have dawdled a whole month in slack laziness about a valuable prize. . . . Expound to us who has the mare, and where and how it is kept; and wait here . . . till the third day from my reaching the place that you may hear that I have either fallen gloriously or returned to your surprise with the spoil!'"

The Northman replied that he had heard before of the boastful nature of the Southerners; he, however, proceeded to tell him that the mare was at Gelligaer, and belonged to *Cadwallon ap Ifor Bach*, Lord of Senghenydd. "By day she feeds in the midst of his troop; at night she stands in the farther corner of his house, with the whole household sleeping between her and the only door, and four of his best men to guard her closely, between her and the fire, on a *brachan* (i.e. a fine carpet); and if you bring that back with you on the mare, ten kine shall be the prize of the mare and five of the carpet." Traer immediately accepted the challenge, and snatching the bridle and the spurs proceeded to the place to see how the ground lay and to prepare his plans. It was a desperate enterprise, for to fail was to be killed on the spot. He kept his eyes and his ears wide open; the night was an ideal one for his purpose, very dark, without a single star showing. Biding his time, he made noiselessly for the door, cut a hole in it with his knife to enable him to get his hand in to open it; then, leaving it wide open, he stole up to the mare and loosed her. Noticing the men asleep on the carpet, he gathered up its long and tough fringes which he tied to the mare's tail, and as he was plunging out, the four were bodily dragged through the huge fire smouldering under its ashes. A hue and cry was immediately raised "and the whole band set out after him, guided only by the sparks which he bore ahead of them in the rug." These he managed to quench and so eluding them was able to reach home safely, where he handed over to the Northman both mare and carpet. He received the promised reward and moreover enhanced the reputation of the Southerners for daring as against the men of the North.

Here, I will give the story not of a horse but of a horse's ears, reminiscent of those of King Midas in a similar Greek myth, which adorned the head of March, Lord of *Castell-March*, and one of King Arthur's soldiers. By wearing some sort of a head-gear resembling a helmet he had been able to hide from every-body, except his barbers, this dread secret. To them, of course, the secret had to be exposed; still he managed to keep it to himself, for he resorted to the expedient of having each one of them put to death lest he should blurt out the truth. In the spot where he buried their bodies there grew an abundance of reeds, and a piper one day going to cut one for his pipe was astounded when he tried it to find that no sound would come through but the astonishing and monotonous repetition of the words: "*March Amheirchion* has horse's ears. *March Amheirchion* has horse's ears!" This was all right in the seclusion of this isolated spot on the moors, it was another thing for the words to be emitted when he played his pipe in the presence of *March Amheirchion*. When he did hear these words he must have been greatly horrified and incensed, but before he proceeded to cut off the piper's head he asked him why he played that tune. The piper replied that the instrument would utter nothing else. *March* then had a try him-self, but as the pipe still continued to repeat the same words, the piper's life was spared. When he discovered where the reed had been cut he realised that the secret was out at last, and the world knew that *March Amheirchion* had horse's ears.

The legend of the dog *Gelert* is the best known of all our legends. At one time it looked as if interest had drifted from the legend to the question of its origin and how, in view of its wide distribution over many countries, it became attached to Bedd Gelert. Welsh writers of a hundred years ago nearly came to blows about it: one, following the example of Walter Map with his *British Book*, gave a version said to have been taken from "an old manuscript," whose existence was promptly and successfully challenged.

In the oldest Welsh version, preserved in the *Iolo MSS.*, there is no prince, but the greyhound, the wolf and the child are there: "There lived formerly at *Abergarwan* a man and wife who had a son . . . an infant in his cradle. One day when his wife had gone to her devotions, the man heard the cry of hounds . . . after a stag. 'I will go and meet them,' said he, 'that I may, as lord of the land, get the share due to me of the stag,' and away he went leaving the child in the cradle, and near the cradle lay his Greyhound. Whilst the man was absent . . . a wolf entered the house, and would have killed and devoured the child; but the Greyhound fought with the wolf, and after a long and bloody struggle, and many wounds and bruises, he succeeded in killing him . . . During the struggle the cradle was . . . overturned. . . . When the man returned . . . the Greyhound, covered with blood, got up to welcome his master. . . . But the man, when he discovered the blood on the Greyhound, and a pool of blood upon the floor, thought that the Greyhound had killed his only child; and so in a fit of rage and distraction, he thrust the Greyhound through with his sword, and killed him. But when he went to the cradle, and had turned it up, and found his child alive and unhurt, and saw the Wolf lying dead, and that the Greyhound had been mangled and torn by the teeth of the Wolf, he became frantic with grief. Hence the proverb: 'Before revenge, first know the cause'. . . . This circumstance gave rise to the following expression: 'As sorry as the man who killed his Greyhound'."

In the Sanskrit parallel a Brahmin, whose wife had gone to perform her purification rite, was left at home with the infant. Soon, there arrived a request from the king for him to attend a religious ceremonial. He decided to go and leave the child in charge of his faithful and pet weasel (ichneumon). Before long a black snake crept in and made for the child. The weasel sprang at it, tore it to pieces and devoured it. When the Brahmin returned the weasel ran to meet him with a great show of affection, its feet and mouth covered with blood. Thinking that it had eaten the child he struck it dead, and ran into the house, only to find the infant unhurt, and the remains all over the place of the black snake; then the whole truth dawned on him and his grief knew no bounds.

In the accepted Welsh version of today the hound was named *Gelert*, and belonged to Prince Llywellyn, great-grandfather of our last Prince, and was a gift from his father-in-law, King John, sent in 1205. When Llywellyn went out hunting one day, *Gelert* failed to answer the hunter's horn, and being his best hound, his absence resulted in a blank day and Llywellyn returned only to find the scene the legend describes.

In this form a ballad version, composed by the Hon. W. R. Spencer, appeared in 1811, and immediately became popular.

The story has been associated with more than one place in Wales, and parallels have been found in Ireland, India, China, Persia and in European countries.

It is, of course, an old Welsh legend whose moral lesson had long become a proverb, but for associating it with Bedd Gelert, grave suspicions rest upon David Pritchard, the landlord of the Royal Goat Hotel, who came there in 1793. It was he, a friend, and the parish clerk, who raised the stone on the spot known as "The Dog's Grave."

The legend of the oldest animals:

Readers of the story of *Kilhwch and Olwen*, in the *Mabinogion*, will remember that in order to win Olwen, the daughter of *Yspaddaden Penkawr*, innumerable enterprises and hazards had to be compassed by the suitor. Kilhwch and his party decided first to seek the release of Mabon, the son of Modron, and in the course of their search they came to the Ousel of *Cilgwri* and asked her if she knew anything of him; she replied that she didn't, but for the sake of King Arthur she would help them, and took them to a representative of an older race of animals, the Stag of *Rhydynvre*. The stag had no information to give either, but to help an embassy from Arthur he took them to the old owl of *Cwm Cawlwyd*. She directed them to an older creature still, the Eagle of *Gwern Abwy*, who in turn directed them to the Salmon of *Llyn Llyw*, the oldest animal of all, who, fortunately, had heard of Mabon; and on the salmon's back Kai and Bedwyr rode up with the tide to Gloucester, where they had an interview with him by the walls of this Severn-side castle.

But there is a similar legend, given in the *Iolo MSS.*, which I am going to give as being the less familiar and also because it has the saving grace of humour, a quality in which early lore and legends may be said to be almost entirely lacking. It is really funny. It is the story of an old eagle—I nearly said an old man—who had become a widower, and had grown tired of his loneliness. He was surrounded by innumerable descendants who were in possession of "all the woods and rocks of the Island of Britain," yet none of them, nor any of his friends, could take the place of his old mate. Sad at heart and depressed in spirit the thought came to him one day that it would be better for him to take unto himself a second wife—and thereby hangs the whole tale.

Despite his depression, he would seem to have kept his eyes open, and to have spotted a likely female in a nearby wood, but he had doubts whether she would do. Strange to say he was not out for a young wife at all. Of course he belonged to, and was the patriarchal head of, a proud race, and the last thing he wished to do was to bring disgrace upon them by debasing the type, or species, which would indeed happen if he married the one he had in mind, for she was an owl! He was really seeking just companionship, and did not wish to bring up another family, since he had already around him his "progeny in countless numbers." Much, if not everything, depended upon her age. Actuated by refined, aquiline feelings, he could not bring himself to ask her point-blank what her age was; possibly, as a very old bird, he knew very well that he would not get the correct answer in any case. There was nothing for it, therefore, but to try to find out from others, so he went round some of the friends and acquaintances of his remote youth.

First of all he flew to the land of Gwent to ask the Stag of *Rhedynfre*, but the stag could not help him, for to him, too, her age had always been a mystery: "Thou seest . . . this oak by which I lie, it is at present no more than an old withered stump, without leaves or branches, but I remember seeing it an acorn on the top of the chief tree of this forest, and it grew into an oak, and an oak is three hundred years in growing, and after that three hundred years in its strength and prime, and after that three hundred years decaying before death, and after death three hundred years returning into earth, and upwards of sixty years of the last hundred of this oak are passed, and the owl has been old since

I first remember her . . . but there is an old friend of mine, who is much older than myself, the Salmon of *Llyn Llifon*, go to him, it is a chance if he does not know something of the age and history of the old owl." And still he was not satisfied! Perhaps these figures, in masses of three hundred years, were too much for him, who even in his youth may not have been good at figures.

Off he went to interview the Salmon, who could only say: "The number of the scales and the spots upon me, and added to these the number of the grains of spawn which I contain, are the number of the years of my age, and to the utmost of my recollection, an old spectre was the Owl, and none of my friends, who were of full age when I was young, either remembered or ever heard anything of the youth of the Owl, nor moreover of her having any children; but there is a companion of mine, who is much older than I, the Ousel of *Cilgwri*, go to him . . . and ask."

The eagle was determined to follow the matter up, now that he had started, so he took another journey and found the Ousel sitting on a little stone: "See here how small this little stone is under me, it is not more than a child of seven years old could take up in his hand, and I have seen it a load for three hundred yoke of the largest oxen, and it never was worn at all, excepting upon my cleansing my beak upon it once every night before going to sleep and striking the point of my wings upon it every morning from the midst of the thorn-bush, and the number of the years of my age are entirely beyond my recollection and notwithstanding that, I never knew the Owl younger to my judgment and observation, according to her appearance, than she is today . . . but there is one a great deal older than I, or, for all I have ever heard, older than my father, and this is the Toad of *Cors Vochno*, in Ceredigion (Cardiganshire), go to him, and if he knows not, I know of none who does."

So once more off he went to have a word with the old toad who in reply to his question said: "I never eat any food save the dust of the earth, and I never eat half enough to satisfy me; see thou those large hills around this bog; where they stand I have seen plain ground; and I have eaten as much earth as they contain, though I eat so little lest the mould of the earth should be consumed before my death. Beyond all memory of mine are the years since I was born, and even the first subject of my recollection; nevertheless much older than I am is the Owl, without the slightest appearance of youth belonging to her, but an old grey hag crying *Ty hwt, Ty hw* (tee-hoot, tee-hoo) in the woods in the long winter nights, frightening the children, and disturbing everybody; and I have no recollection, nor did I ever hear of her having children, but what I saw myself, old hags far beyond the age of bearing children were the youngest of her daughters, and her granddaughters and her great-granddaughters."

The toad was forthright, helpful and, as it turned out, convincing, but he certainly was uncomplimentary: "a old grey hago" but then, if the eagle was hurt, he had only himself to blame, for he had never told him that he meant to make her his bride. One ought not perhaps to expect anything better from a toad.

At last the old bird was satisfied and "saw he could marry her, and take her for a mate, without bringing on his tribe debasement or disgrace, degradation or degeneration." The legend goes on to say that it was "from the courtship of the old eagle it was known which were the oldest creatures in the world . . . the Eagle of *Gwernabwy*, the Stag of *Rhedynfre*, the Salmon of *Llyn Llifon*, the Ousel of *Cilgwri*, the Toad of *Cors Vochno* and the Owl of *Cwmcawlyd*, and there is not save the ridge of land older than they."

The legend is a very old one: Dafydd ap Gwilym in his poem, *Yr Oed*, refers to a version, naming only three animals, which is older still, and which is known in many lands. It came "to Europe originally from India." For comparisons of the Welsh with the Eastern versions, see *Y Cymmrodor* (1882), p. 169.

Writers on Wales, generally tourists of the eighteenth century, often refer, in some surprise, to the number of goats that they saw in the countryside; indeed, the Welshman was always associated with his goat as the Irishman with his pig. It was very natural, for it was a popular animal, and it survived as an adjunct to cottage life, like the pig and the poultry, well into the twenties of this century—in fact, until the advent of the cheap milk scheme for schools and the general expansion of the milk service into the country—due entirely to the appearance of the milk-lorry and the milk-van. The goat was an animal easily and economically kept, it needed hardly any attention at all, and for its size gave a surprisingly large amount of milk, entirely free from the tuberculosis germ. Giraldus Cambrensis in his journey through Wales with Archbishop Baldwin, in 1188, notes that the wooded hills were full of goats and swine and herds. Descendants of these herds may have run wild on the mountains to within almost living memory. As late as 1869 two wild goats were shot on the Prescelly Mountains—one, a pure white, whose horns measured along the outer curve $36\frac{1}{2}$ inches, and the distance between tip and tip of the two horns measured, in a straight line across, 39 inches. The other was a black one and an equally fine specimen. Abergavenny and district became noted for its herds of goats and, besides being a centre for the manufacture of wigs (from goats' hair), became, also, a centre for the cure of tuberculosis—whey made from goat's milk.

The decay of superstition and the advent of fuller veterinary knowledge may have also something to do with the disappearance of the goat, for during my early days on the farm many farmers kept a billy-goat to run with their herds as a preventive of abortion; on some farms more faith was put in the donkey for that purpose.

Despite their wide distribution I do not think any of them acquired notoriety or became the subject of a legend except the goat of Cadwalader. It was well known to Shakespeare, for in reply to Fluellen's demand that he should eat the leek, which had been the subject of disparaging remarks on his part, Pistol refuses: "No. Not for Cadwalader, and all his goats." (Henry V, Act v, Scene i.)

Goats were believed to be on good terms with the fairies who on Friday nights combed their beards to make them look nice for Sunday. Black goats were keepers of treasures, and the presence of one indicated the burial somewhere near of hidden money.

But to return to Cadwalader. "Cadwalader owned a very handsome goat named Jenny, of which he was extremely fond

"Ah, Cadwalader, Have I at last found you?"

and which seemed equally fond of him." But one day, like one possessed, she suddenly took to her heels and made for the mountains, with Cadwalader after her as fast as he could go. As may well be imagined, a man chasing a goat over steep and rough paths in the mountains cannot be expected to be in the best of tempers, so he picked up a stone and threw it after her. His aim was sure and Jenny was knocked clean over a precipice to her doom. Cadwalader descended the rock to where she lay, not quite dead, for she was still breathing, and indeed had the strength to lift her head and kiss his hand, an act which so affected him that he burst into tears. He sat down to try to comfort her, with her head on his lap. As he lay there nursing the dying goat, the moon rose, in the light of which he saw that "the goat had become transformed into a beautiful young woman, whose brown eyes, as her head lay on his arm, looked into his in a very disturbing way. 'Ah, Cadwalader,' said she, 'have I at last found you?'"

This greatly upset Cadwalader, for he was a married man of settled ways and principles, but when the maiden arose and offered him her hand he found himself accepting it, and together, hand in hand, they went, climbing over the mountains again. As they went along he could not help thinking that though her hand was soft, it felt more like a hoof than a hand. Presently they came to the top of a very high mountain where they were surrounded by a large company of shadowy goats, which all began bleating and making a most unearthly din.

One who seemed to hold the position of king and ruler over them had a particularly powerful voice; he entertained no friendly feelings towards Cadwalader, but rushing at him "and butting him in the stomach, sent him toppling over a crag, as he had sent his own poor nanny-goat." The following morning when he came to himself, the sun was up and the birds were singing, but he never again saw his nanny-goat, nor the fair maiden she was changed into.

Another goat figures in one of the modern legends that have gathered round that famous and saintly person, Vicar Pritchard, of Llandovery. When legends begin to gather round a person it is a sure sign that he fills a big place in the estimate and affections of the common people.

The legend goes that the old Vicar in the early days of his ministry was entirely without a sense of vocation, a waster and a drunkard. He possessed a very friendly goat which accompanied him regularly to the public-houses. One night he gave her beer to drink, which the goat thought tasted good and drank more than was good for her. When closing time came a drunken goat led by a drunken clergyman made their way home as best they could. The following night the Vicar again called a drink for his friend the goat, but she would not have it; turning her head away in disgust as much as to say, "I have been drunk once and I never want to be again."

This so affected the Vicar that from that moment he never touched another drop, but turned over a new leaf and became one of our most exemplary priests.

It is all very well to say that one ought to know that it is not true, but are any of our legends true! I give it merely as a specimen of what peasant Wales believed in; especially did a large number like to believe it as typical of the parish priest. If anyone desires a complete refutation let him read *Y Ficar Prichard* by D. Gwenallt Jones.

Much lore has gathered round the cuckoo: many believed, as they did of the swallow, that it did not migrate but slept in some suitable hole, often in a tree; and many instances are related of its waking up in the heat of the fire—when the particular tree in which it was hibernating was cut down for fire-wood—mistaking its warmth for the coming of spring, and uttering its call once again. Farmers did not like to hear the cuckoo until the trees were in full leaf. If it came before that they repeated in ominous accents, *gwerth dy geffyl, a phryn dy bwn*—sell thy horse and buy thy sackful—meaning, presumably, reduce thy stock and buy feeding-stuff.

There was a proverb to the effect that, of all the evils of early things, the worst was an early cuckoo: *Gwaethaf cynnar, cynnar côg*. A late cuckoo again boded nothing but scarcity and want. *Gwcw glame, cosyn dime* (literally, a May cuckoo, a ha'penny cheese).

Much depended on where one was when one heard the cuckoo first: if in a field, well covered with grass, then one could look forward to an abundance of milk and butter and cheese; if on the other hand one stood on a fallow field, or on the road, one could only expect a scarcity of such things as the fields produced. If without money in one's pocket, so would one be throughout the year—many a countryman took care at that time of the year that he was not caught unawares. The worst misfortune befell those who heard it in bed, for it meant that in the course of the year there would be much sickness and much lying in bed.

A very beautiful legend is preserved by George Owen, the Elizabethan historian of Pembrokeshire, and is connected with the cuckoo's arrival at the church of Nevern in the north of the county. On April 7th, the patronal festival in that church, dedicated to St. Brynach, a saint of the sixth century, the parish priest would never begin to say Mass until the cuckoo had arrived; for, time out of mind, it had always arrived on that day, perching on the famous stone of St. Brynach, in the churchyard. This stone, by the way, standing 13 feet high, and richly carved and ornamented with interlacing patterns on each of its four sides, is one of the finest specimens we possess of a celtic cross.

One year the bird was late in arriving, and priest and people waited patiently. After long waiting it came and settled on the stone, but in so obviously weak and worn out a condition that it was scarcely able to utter the first note before it dropped dead. I can well imagine the distress of the poor bird as it battled with the storms that raged over the Pyrenees, saying to itself: "I must get through, tomorrow is St. Brynach's day, and I must be at Nevern. I have never failed before, nor any of my ancestors before me, for to our family has been given for generations the honour of starting the Mass on this day in the church of the holy Brynach. I must not fail." Nor did it!

The owl and the wren: The owl is a somewhat dreaded bird in Wales, probably on account of its nocturnal and furtive habits. It emerges silently from its perch in an ivy-covered tree and glides past one without a sound as if it were a spirit: nor is its call particularly attractive. The wren on the other hand is held in high regard—who could help holding in admiration a small bird which brings up so large a family and builds such a cosy nest for them? It may be, too, that that noisy, perky, bossy spiritedness with which he stands up for himself has something to do with it.

But he was not always popular. Back in the days of the Druids, who presided over the courts of justice, if their verdict was questioned, they replied that the wren had disclosed the whole truth of the matter to them—and the testimony of the wren was final. Bit by bit the people grew to hate the wren and he was cruelly hunted and decimated.

In a contest amongst the birds to decide who should be their king, and that honour to go to the one who could fly the highest, the wren figures in a role characteristic of his impudence and audacity. He perched quietly and unnoticed on the back of the eagle, and as that bird ascended majestically far above all the others and was on the point of being acclaimed monarch of the air, the cheeky little wren flew off his back and, mounting a few yards higher than the exhausted eagle, robbed him of the honour. The eagle naturally was most indignant and in his wrath fell upon him as he came down, and hurled him to the ground. The wren was not greatly hurt, but he lost half the feathers of his tail, and that is why he has ever since been known as *Y Dryw Bach Cwta*—the cutty-tailed wren.

In another version the eagle is shown as having easily won and from the heights proclaimed himself king, when to his surprise he heard a small piping voice above him saying, "No. No. Not yet." From the safety of these few yards above, it challenged the eagle to "come up here," but he was too exhausted, and the wren became king. When the birds discovered who their king was, such a sense of shame possessed them that they immediately met in secret conclave to decide what to do about it, for the situation was intolerable. It was solemnly decided that the new "king" would have to die, but the form of death by which he was to pay the penalty for his impudence was apparently not discussed. It occurred to them, however, that as their tears were so copious it would be best to drown him in them. For this purpose a pan was procured into which each bird "wept" its tears; when the turn of the owl came, this clumsy creature, mounting the edge, upset the pan and spilled all the accumulated tears. This so enraged the other birds that they set on him, and that is why they still mob him to this day. Hardly ever does he dare to show his face before they have all retired to sleep.

In yet another version it is said that the wren injured himself in falling and that the birds prepared a healing broth for him, each one adding some ingredient to the pot. This is the vessel the owl is said to have upset and so enraged the birds.

Chapter Eleven

HIDDEN TREASURES

FAIRY GOLD

AMONGST the earliest stories that I listened to were those connected with buried treasure—usually crocks of gold —and what happened to those who tried to get it. Many large tumuli, crugs and cairns were pointed out to me as having been at some time or other opened, and many cromlechs and menhirs as having been dug under, but the result was always the same—an immediate outbreak of thunder and lightning of such severity that operations had to cease at once and safety sought.

It was generally believed that the fairies had a lot of wealth hidden away in their underground homes. Opinion was divided as to how they got possession of their treasures, especially gold currency: some said there was no mystery about it at all—"they were thieves without their equal." Others maintained that they got them because of their power to sense the presence of lost or forgotten hoards.

I have already, in describing their underground abodes, referred to *Ynys Geinon* rock, in Swansea valley, where there was an entrance, guarded by a huge stone, to an underground passage which led all the way to *Craig Y Nos*, the residence of the late Adelina Patti. A servant man from one of the neighbouring farms, while out shooting rabbits near the spot, happened to say the word used by the fairies in entering and leaving, when lo, and behold! the stone rose of itself. He entered, and descended by a gold ladder of twenty-one or twenty-two rungs. As he did not know the correct word to bring the stone back again on the entrance, the down-rush of draught, putting out all the candles, indicated at once to the little folk that something was wrong. He was discovered and kept with them for seven years; at the end of that time he escaped, taking with him a hatful of guineas. As he had now discovered the pass-words, in and out, as well as the hidden hoards of gold, he passed the information on to a neighbouring farmer, who also went down and brought up "thrice the fill of a salt-chest, of guineas, half-guineas, and seven-and-sixpenny pieces in one day."

He was not satisfied with this haul but went again, and this time was caught. "It is said that his four quarters hang in a room under the castle."

Hundreds of tons of gold had been accumulated by the fairies "under *Mynydd y Drum*" (now called Onllwyn), some of which a local "conjurer" or wizard, a man with an iron hand (*dyn llawharn*), said he would get if only he could get hold of a man plucky enough to spend a night with him there. He found one in John Gethin. They started operations, whether on the spot or elsewhere we are not told, but first of all the wizard "traced two rings on the sward touching each other 'like the number 8'," into one of which the wizard entered, and John Gethin into the other. The wizard charged Gethin not to go out of the ring whatever happened, and then "proceeded to *trafod 'i lyfrau* or 'busy himself with his books'; and there soon appeared a monstrous bull, bellowing dreadfully, but the plucky Gethin held his ground and the bull vanished." Next, a most terrifying object, in the form of a "fly-wheel of fire," appeared, and made a straight dive for poor Gethin and caused him to swerve out of the ring. The wheel then assumed its proper form, that of the devil, and in this guise he began to drag Gethin away.

Realising that the first thing to do was to get Gethin back into the ring, the wizard, too, seized him, but the devil was the stronger and was fast getting the upper hand. As the devil was now the master of the situation the wizard begged of him to let him keep Gethin while the piece of candle he had in his hand lasted. The devil consented and let go of Gethin, whereupon the wizard immediately blew out the candle to the utter discomfiture of his adversary.

Gethin preserved that piece of candle very carefully, keeping it in a specially cool place, yet despite all his care it continued to waste away. He took to his bed, and as the candle wasted so did he; both came to an end simultaneously. Nothing was left of either. To save appearances on the day of the funeral a lump of clay was substituted for the body. Thus ended the attempt to get some of the "hundreds of tons of gold" accumulated under *Mynydd y Drum*.

As a change, there comes from Caernarvonshire a story not of a hoard of gold but of a golden chair: "There was once a beautiful girl, the daughter of hard-working parents who held a farm on the side of the hill, and their handsome industrious daughter took care of the sheep." At certain times of the year she visited the sheep daily, but never did she go without her knitting needles; she was so experienced and proficient a knitter now that she could knit as she walked, which I have myself seen many a Welsh-woman doing. The fairies had long noticed her industry, and in the goodness of their hearts must have decided to show their appreciation of it, for one day when she lifted her eyes from her knitting she was surprised to see in front of her a beautiful golden chair. She went up to it; yes, it was real enough, but it was so massive that she could not move it. This was a grave matter, for she knew that whatever the fairies gave had to be taken possession of without delay. Here she was, right away on a wild mountain-side, far from home and without anybody near to help her. What could she do? Could she find her way to it again? Then all of a sudden the thought came to her that if she tied the end of the yarn she had with her to the chair and unrolled the ball as she made her way home she could easily find the way to it the follow-

ing day. And this she did—until the ball came to an end, then she
tied the yarn in the knitted stocking to it and walked on. In time
that too came to an end. She had come to within a short distance
of her home and could now see the folk moving about; she
shouted to them but they took no notice. She decided to put a
stone on the end of the wool and run home as fast as she could.
Her parents went back with her at once to the stone, but no stone
or yarn could they find, though they searched and searched until
it was quite dark. The following day they went to search again,
combing carefully that part of the mountain where she had been
the day before, but to no avail. Had that yarn been long enough,
that beautiful chair would have been hers. As it is, it is still hidden
in the mountain, and is intended for somebody, but it is no use
anyone going to look for it, for to that person "fated to possess
it" it will be revealed one day "as if by accident."

I am always glad to get hold of a story with a touch of humour
in it, and one such is told of a certain John Davies, a painter, but
once a carpenter, and a very considerable musician, who never
moved without his flute. One October, "about the year 1860,"
he was returning, late, from Aberayron, over the uplands of
Cardiganshire, and in order to push on, passed all the public-
houses until he came to one 3 miles from home; here he went in
to seek "strength and courage to meet the ghosts" that he might
meet, now that it was getting later still. Off he went again, guided
over the moor by the one hedge that lined the road. By and by
he saw a light which he took to be coming from the cottage of
old Peggi of *Ty Clottas*; this he followed until he became somewhat suspicious, as now and again it "gave a little jump."

Early next morning Peggi awoke to the sound of light and
merry music, and upon going out to investigate, saw "to her
great surprise . . . a man sitting on a heap, blowing into some
instrument." She shouted and asked him what he wanted there,
the man seemed to "wake up" and, giving her a scowling and
nasty look, replied, "Ah you—you have spoiled everything; it
nearly came to a bargain."

A friend getting to hear of this asked him what it was that Peggi
had spoilt. John told the whole story: how he had strayed on to

the moor, had chanced on a fairy ring "where a large number of little fairy ladies danced," all "very beautiful, but small, and wearing short white dresses coming down to the knees only." To his surprise one of them took his arm and started dancing with him. After a bit the queen herself appeared and asked him where he came from, and what he was. He replied that he was a painter, but the queen did not seem to be in the least interested in painters, for she merely remarked that fairies had no need of painters. John was, however, a man of parts and though as a painter he had failed to impress, he was also a musician, and proceeded to entertain the company on the flute, with Irish, Scotch and English airs; this not only failed to impress but failed to please, for he was told they were fairies of Welsh descent. He at once proceeded to make up for his inexcusable omission, "to their great delight, and they had a merry time of it." Second impressions were being created which were much more favourable towards him, but he spoilt it all by asking for a glass of beer, only to be drily informed that they were all "teetotals."

He fell in love with one of the pretty maidens and asked the queen for her hand, adding in self-recommendation that he had at home "a horse named Bob." Surely the possession of a horse would be a great recommendation, but to have a horse of the name of Bob would make it irresistible. What picture the lady formed of Bob it is difficult to imagine, for it would be impossible to think of a name that could convey less; anyhow there it was, not merely a horse, but a horse of the name of Bob! It was not the only possession he could boast of; he also had a cart—and of "his own making"! Now this does convey a picture; I have seen some carts on the roads in my time, but I doubt whether I have seen anything that could be compared with that which would be produced by a carpenter turned painter—and a workman who leaves his trade does so invariably because he is no good at it. Perhaps it was a cart made long ago for a local farmer who when he saw it refused to take it, offering in lieu of payment the advice—which was taken—that the sooner he turned tailor or painter the better. The queen must have been a shrewd as well as a polite little woman, for she made no comment, but it is obvious she was not impressed; in view, however, of his ability as a musician she would give her consent provided that he and his wife came once a month, when the moon was full, to visit them. She then "took hold of a pot of gold" to give him as a dowry, but just as he was stretching forth his hands to take it, "old Peggi *Ty Clottas*, came to shout and to spoil the whole thing, for as soon as the fairy ladies saw old Peggi, they all vanished . . . into the underground" and the owner of Bob, and of the cart of his own making, never saw them or the pot of gold again.

The next story comes from the mountains of Merionethshire: A weaver by the name of David, on the way to Bala, was met "on the top of the *Garn* by two fairies who desired him to follow them, promising if he would do so, that they would show him a chest filled with gold." As a poor man nothing suited him better and he went with them; eventually they descended from the bare mountain into a secluded glen where he was shown the chest of gold. The poor weaver was delighted; his only problem now was how to get it from there, for like the girl in the story of the golden chair, he also had heard that whatever the fairies gave had to be taken possession of at once. Like the chair it was too heavy to carry away, for the fairies, when they gave, gave generously— too generously sometimes, with whatever purpose we may only guess, for the reader will notice in these stories that time and again the gift or treasure is lost because it was too heavy to move. All that David could do now was to stake his claim by thrusting his stick down into the gold. He then started for home, not altogether happy about the matter, and as he emerged from the glen he looked back. Yes, the chest was there all right and his stick in it. Bala went completely out of his mind, his one anxiety now was to get home as quickly as he could and break the good news to his wife. As it was then late, there was nothing they could do that night, and David turned to some task, having very solemnly warned her not to breathe a word to anybody. But the news was too wonderful to keep and while her husband was away she rushed across to her next-door neighbour and told her everything—even that she and her husband were going to fetch it in the morning. What was exchanged between two women might not have mattered much, but sitting next to her was her husband, the miller—a shrewd man. When the two got next day to the mountain the chest had gone—and the stick. Soon enough there came abundant evidence that the miller and his family had come to a great fortune.

There is a tradition that a young man went to the recesses of the mountains in the neighbourhood of *Lake Ogwen* and discovered there a cave, in which there was a large quantity of brazen vessels of every shape and description. In his joy he sprang to take hold of one of them, but *och!* it was too heavy to move. There was nothing for it, therefore, but to leave it all and return the next day with a friend. He closed the mouth of the cave and was on the point of coming away when he suddenly remembered how he had often heard of people losing treasures by failing to find their way back to them again. After thinking for a long time he hit upon quite a clever idea; he would, as he went home, chip the stick he carried, and let the chips drop; they would mark the path all the way back. Before he reached home he had chipped away the whole stick, but he had come near enough. The next morning he and his friend started off early, but when they came to where the chips should have started they failed to find any, for "the fairies had been there and gathered them all up."

It is said that it is a *Gwyddel* (an Irishman) who will one day get this treasure—and this is how it will come about: "A *Gwyddel* will one day come to these parts as a shepherd, and in the course of one of his journeys to the mountain to watch the sheep—when fate shall see fit—a black, speckled-headed sheep will run before him and make for this cave. He will run after it and upon his entry into it, to his great astonishment, he will see these treasures and will take them away. In this manner, it is said, the possessions of the *Gwyddelod* (the Irish) will be restored to them in some age or other." One could quote many stories in which the chipped stick figures.

There is a local tradition that Merlin, when he left *Dinas Emrys*, in Snowdonia, put all his treasures in a large golden vessel, which, together with his golden chair, he hid in a cave in the city, and then rolled a huge stone on to its mouth, covering the whole place over with earth and green turf so that no one could possibly find them.

As the treasures in the cave by *Llyn Ogwen* are one lucky day to be possessed by an Irish shepherd lad, so Merlin's are to be the possession at some time or other of a "golden-haired and blue-eyed stripling," and "when he draws nigh to Dinas Emrys, a bell will ring to invite him into the cave, which will open out of its own accord as soon as his foot touches it."

Many in the district imagined themselves to be this blue-eyed, golden-haired youth; one family in particular entertained great hopes, for in addition to the possession of all the physical requirements, a ghostly visitor came annually to one of the sons urging him to follow him, but he had not sufficient courage. A nephew, however, had and on one occasion thought that the treasure was actually coming to him: "One night . . . when passing the Dinas about midnight—the hour appointed for the rightful heir to enter into his inheritance—when right opposite the middle of the hill, he thought he heard a bell ringing." He stopped, it rang again; he imagined, too, he could hear a voice saying "Come here," and the bell rang again. He leaped over the wall and followed the sound through woods, copses and other obstacles in the dark until, getting quite close to it, the ringing ceased under a well-known ridge. He made straight for the ridge, but when he got there "a black hand-fed calf gave a leap and darted by him, furiously rattling an old bell which hung by a cord around its neck."

Some foolish people pushed into the cave of *Ogof Dafydd Siencyn*, in Nant Conway, and saw a huge oak chest, strengthened with iron bands, on which stood an enormous billy-goat which watched them and turned its aged head as it followed their movements.

Two shepherd brothers in the parish of Llanllechid, in North Wales, one day climbed the *Benglog* to look for their sheep and there, in an unfrequented place, the younger saw a hole in the ground, leading to a cave, in the midst of which stood a round table and on it heaps of gold and silver. He dare not go in to fetch any of it, because there stood near it a greyhound watching him through eyes of fire, and ready to pounce on him. When he told his brother about it they both decided to enter together, but they failed to find it again despite their diligent search.

Under Castell Coch, near Cardiff, down in a deep vault, there is an iron chest, containing the treasures of Ifor Bach, a very noted Welsh chieftain of Norman times. Three huge eagles, described as being "fierce birds . . . having dark grey plumage . . . eyes . . . large and brilliantly red, with a light that flashes like fiendish lightning through the gloom of the cavern," guard it. Between October and March they create a fearful commotion—"they scream and shriek, causing terror in the countryside." Efforts have been made to destroy them: In the seventeenth century a party "armed from head to foot" were savagely attacked and glad to make their escape. Another whose arms had been blessed by a priest met a similar fate.

In the eighteenth century trained veterans who had seen service abroad and armed "with pistols and cutlasses" went down, but they, too, were set upon with the utmost ferocity and as they made their way out "the eagles screamed in exultation, while the flapping of their wings sounded like distant thunder." No person or armed body has been able to dislodge them, for they are there to guard the treasures until Ifor Bach returns again and with him "his twelve hundred men of Glamorgan."

I wonder whether, if legends had not ceased when they did, Ifor Bach was in process of supplanting *Owen Lawgoch* as *Owen* had earlier supplanted King Arthur?

HUMAN HOARDS

More often than not, however, it was a solitary ghost that revealed the whereabouts of hidden or forgotten hoards of gold. Ghosts were generally supposed to be of three kinds: (1) spirits of the dead; (2) spirits of the living; and (3) goblins or demons. The ghosts of murdered men walked about until they could find someone brave enough to speak to them, so that they might reveal their secret to them; then they vanished. There also walked

Guarding the Treasure of Ifor Bach

about the ghosts of people who had died suddenly and intestate, and who returned to protest against the misuse, the unjust retention, or distribution, of their money. Misers were believed not to be able to rest in their graves because their gold "weighed on their bones," so they came back to ease their load by revealing the place where their hoard was hidden. The motive of reappearance was generally connected with hidden money; if not, some neglected duty.

Though it was to their late friends and relatives that ghosts usually appeared, they sometimes came to perfect strangers. The hour of their visitation was between midnight and cock-crow, when they departed. It was the aim of everybody therefore to be home before that time, nor would anyone happily start a journey before cock-crow. Christmas Eve was the only night when no spirits were permitted to be abroad. If two persons were together, to only one would a ghost appear and speak, but it would not speak unless it was first spoken to, for when a person died his tongue was doomed to eternal silence, and only the act of being addressed could lift the ban. Had mortals always understood this, much delay, and the annoyance of repeated visits, could have been avoided, for their persistence indicated the urgency of their message. "Their presence was sometimes announced by a clanking of chains, by shrieks or other horrible noises, and dogs and horses trembled and perspired at their presence," but usually they just appeared unheralded.

The person visited had, therefore, to speak first, and that after a well-established formula, invoking in the first place the name of the Trinity; then its business had to be demanded—the question to be repeated three times, unless the ghost recovered the power of speech earlier and rendered it unnecessary. Neglect to carry out instructions purposely or unwittingly led to dire consequences and there are on record cases of severe buffeting and man-handling. Questions about its present state gave the gravest offence.

When the ghosts had delivered their message they were then ready for their release and the severance of the last link that bound them to earth. There are recorded instances where this has taken place there and then, leaping flames consuming them on the spot; the mortal creature who had been their agent in recovering the treasure being requested to turn his back while this process was taking place, and charged on no account to look round, possibly to prevent any mental shock or it may be that nothing should mar a complete and expeditious dissolution.

It was, as I said, popularly believed that a spirit could not rest if it had hidden any hoarded money, but in the case of the ghost of Morgan Lewis, a weaver, which appeared to Walter John Harry who now occupied his old house in the Ebbw valley, it was "bottoms of wool." Walter John Harry, lying awake in his bed one night, and in great fear as he heard the ghost of the weaver coming up the stairs, "bearing a candle in his hand," asked him, "Morgan Lewis . . . why dost thou walk this earth?" The reply was that until those "bottoms of wool hidden in the wall . . . were removed it could not sleep." The inference was that the wool had been stolen. Charged not to disturb the house again, it vanished.

The river Ogmore in Glamorgan was a favourite river with ghosts, and all hoards directed by them to be cast away were ordered to be thrown into this river—and always *with* the stream.

Barbara, the wife of Edward, the tailor of Llantwit Major, was "a hale and hearty woman until a secret pressed sorely upon her mind." Her mother-in-law, "Mollans, as the old woman was called" had entrusted her with her savings and had charged her to share it equally amongst several members of the family. Barbara, however, decided to keep it all for herself, but the spirit of old Mollans was not going to take a thing like that lying down, so up she rose and returned, pinching Barbara at night and keeping her awake, until she became quite ill. At last she gave in, but rather than divide it amongst the family as originally directed, she consented to throw it into the Ogmore. "The spirit then led her out of the house and wafted her so high in the air that she saw the church . . . and all the houses far below her. In her flurry she threw the bag of money up the stream instead of down with it, whereupon the spirit [old Mrs. Mollans, be it remembered] in a great rage, and with a savage look, tossed her into a whirlwind!"

She was later found by the bellringers in a lane, "wet and bedraggled and her hair filled with sand."

Though she had survived the whirlwind, and the drop, without, apparently, receiving any permanent injury, she never had any more peace in her life: "supernatural noises and knockings were always heard in the house." Barbara became so nervous in the end that she would not open the door to anyone, imagining the knocking to be that of Mrs. Mollans; but one day the spirit of old Mrs. Mollans, which was not going to be kept down, assumed the shape of a crow and came down the chimney or flew in at an open window. Some time later a real crow flew in at the window and flapped its wings about Barbara's head. She screamed in terror, bringing in all the neighbours, who wanted to destroy it, but Barbara shouted, "Don't. Don't! If you kill the crow, you will kill my mother-in-law, and I shall go to perdition."

How an old Glamorgan family got their Money: A young girl engaged by a farmer's wife became very unsettled and wanted to leave; on being asked the reason, she replied that whenever she went alone along a nearby lane a strange man always met her—and always at dusk, or at night, never in the moonlight. Her master advised her to ask him what he wanted; this she plucked up courage to do, with the result that she was asked to come again the following night and bring a spade with her, but to tell no one. The next night came and the stranger pointed to a spot in a corner of the field and told her to dig there. She did so and found a pot "containing a large number of gold coins." The stranger further told her that "so long as she kept seven of the coins and handed them down to posterity, there would be good luck in the family."

Soon after this her mistress died and a year later she became her master's second wife. Again the stranger came and charged her once more to see that seven coins were handed down; if that was done the farm would always remain in their possession. If any of them were squandered their possessions would be reduced by that proportion. The family took great care of the sovereigns and became the owners of a large estate. One spendthrift later squandered his wealth and parted with five of them. His son, however, managed to get hold of the other two and emigrating to America made a large fortune. "His descendants had great pleasure in visiting the old farm in Glamorgan, associated with the origin of their wealth."

Solitary hawthorn trees were supposed to mark the site of hidden gold. Long ago there was one such in a Glamorgan field near Llantrisant, and a man living nearby thought he would try to get the treasure underneath. He had first "to gather some springwort and forget-me-not flowers and leaves, and make them into a girdle, which had to be worn around the waist next to the skin. A sprig each of the herb and flower were to be worn in the hat. In this way the man went to seek the treasure. A condition to be fulfilled was that each time treasure was taken away, the sprigs of the herb and flower worn in the hat were to be left as an acknowledgement of the transaction." The man went to work and dug down till he came to a large cavern and here "beyond some bones" he found the gold. He continued to carry away from the vast treasure for some months and became very rich; on one occasion, however, his load being heavier than usual, he forgot to leave the symbols of acknowledgement—and he never found the spot again; indeed he never "could remember in which field the old hawthorn grew."

Sometimes ghosts were very considerate and gave helpers something for their trouble: the ghost of David Pritchard, the thrifty and prosperous landlord of the Goat Hotel, Beddgelert, when demanded by his old servant why he wandered "about in the night in this fashion," replied, "Hwlyn, I am glad to see thee, because my bones could not rest in the grave. Go and tell Alice tomorrow to raise up the hearthstone of the bar-room, and she will find there two hundred guineas, two of which she must give thee."

At what speed ghosts travel and take their human agents with them we can only guess, but it must be supersonic, for a young man, the son of an innkeeper in the parish of Ystradgynlais, was asked to go so far as Philadelphia, in America, to dispose of some treasure. The story is told by the Reverend Edmund Jones.

The ghost appeared to him "in the shape of a well-dressed woman who stood before him in a narrow lane. He strove to pass her, and did in much fear, as doubting what she might be." Some time after he saw her again in the same shape at the same place and in the same dress. "He was afraid to pass by her: but he was resolved to speak to her, and asked her what she wanted with him. She told him he must go to Philadelphia, in Pennsylvania, and take a box from a house there, which she described (in which there was two hundred pounds) and charged him to meet her on the Friday night following." He mentioned this to some friends and it reached the ears of the curate of the parish who immediately called a prayer meeting. It was noticed that the young man was very uneasy. After the meeting was over he went with the parson's servants to the stables, and on coming from there was snatched up by the ghost, who was very angry. He was severely reprimanded for telling her business to others and for failing to come to meet her as arranged; this was not all, she carried him away to a river and threw him in! However, she "bid him not to be afraid, that she would not hurt him, because she had not charged him not to speak of her charge to meet her on Friday night; but that he should not have gone to the parson's house. Now, said she, we begin the journey: He was then lifted up and carried away he knew not how, and when he came to the place, he was taken into a house, and then conducted to a fine room: the spirit then bid him lift up a board, which he did; he then saw the box and took it; then the spirit said he must go three miles and cast it into the Black Sea; they went as he thought to a lake of clear water where he was commanded to throw the box into it; which when he did there was such a noise as if all about was going to pieces. From thence he was taken up and carried to the place where he was first taken up." He was three days and three nights on this mysterious journey and could hardly speak when he arrived home, but he managed to ask her one important question: was he then free, and she replied "yes." Asked by his friends what she looked like, he replied that "she was largely made, looked pale, her looks severe and her voice hollow, different from a human voice."

A very quaint but dramatic story is given by Elizabeth Williams in her book *Siaced Fraith*, published by *Gwasg Aberystwyth* (1952). She says that such stories were very well known eighty years ago and were often recited by young men in stable lofts, and formed an important part of the *noson lawen*—a form of rural entertainment.

The following is the story of the *Bwgan Coch Bach*—The Little Red Bogy-man: Many years ago a farmer's son, dissatisfied with his lot, made up his mind to try to better himself. He took his wallet, collected all his money, and armed only with a stout ashen stick—which stood him in good stead in his encounters with highwaymen—began his journey. He travelled for weeks without success, putting up at night at the various farms, where he always found great kindness. One day, at night-fall, at the end of a long and tedious journey, he found himself in a strange country, with only one distant house in sight, for which he made. He knocked at the door and asked the goodman of the house for a night's lodging. The house, he was told, was full and the only thing the owner could offer him was permission to sleep in a nearby house, out of sight in the wood. He himself and his family spent every day there and there was a nice cosy fire there—he was very welcome to go there. As for food, he could be provided with that to take with him. It was only fair, however, that he should tell him that not one of his family nor any of his servants would sleep there, because some spirit caused a disturbance there. "Very well," said the young man, "I shall be pleased to stay there. I am not afraid of spirits because I never did wrong to anyone at any time."

He went forward through the wood and into the house. Having enjoyed his supper he sat down by the huge fire to meditate upon the events of the day. The silence soothed his tired frame and he felt extraordinarily contented.

There was a noise! What was it that was knocking?—and in the chimney! It was followed by a voice—growing louder and louder —"I am coming down. I am coming down. I am coming down." In the end the young man lost his patience and shouted, "Come down then and be hanged to you." And down from the chimney came a little man about 3 feet high, red from head to heel—his shoes, his clothes and his skin, all flaming red. "Was it necessary to make all that noise?" asked the young man. "You are not much of a thing." "Oh," replied the little red man, "if *I* am small, two bigger than me will come in after me," and with that the door opened and two huge bony men came in carrying a coffin—one at each end—which they deposited on two chairs.

"Go outside until I call you," ordered the little man, and turning to the young man, continued: "Come with me." "No, I won't," said the young man. The little man repeated his command, "Come with me." "Well," replied the young man, "in case you think I am afraid of you, I will," and followed him. They came to steps leading down to a kind of cellar. "Go down," commanded the little red man again. "No, I won't," said the lad, "go yourself." He repeated his command, but the lad persisted, "No, I won't." "For the last time I am directing you to go down." "Oh, well," replied the lad, "in case you think I am afraid of you, I will," and down he went, with the little red man following.

After they had reached the bottom, the little man said: "You did wisely to obey; if you hadn't, your body would have been in that coffin and that would have been the end of you. Now lift this stone." The young man obeyed at once, and underneath they found a huge chest full of gold. "I have waited for you for years," said the little red bogy, "to put right a great wrong I once did. It was I who called you from your home. You are to divide this gold with the man who allowed you to stay here, and he is to give you this house and the farm-land around it. And so you can live happily all your life. If one of you acts unfairly, the body of the one who does so will be in that coffin you saw, and he will not be seen again. I will come again tomorrow night— and woe betide you if there has not been a fair division—and now don't look round." With that he vanished.

At day-break the owner and his servants came, very anxious to know how the young man had fared. They knocked at the door—there was no reply. "We must break the door in," shouted the man, "the young man must have been killed." The noise woke him up and he came down and told them all the happenings of the previous night. The man agreed at once to act in accordance with the directions of the little red man. The young man established himself in the house and in time married the daughter of the owner. They lived happily throughout their lives and the *Bwgan Coch Bach* was never seen nor heard again.

BIBLIOGRAPHY

BIBLIOGRAPHY

Vitæ Sanctorum Britanniæ Et Genealogiæ.
A. Wade-Evans. Welsh University Press.

The Cambro-Briton. Vol. ii.

Cymru Fu: Hanesion, Traddodiadau . . . Chwedlau a Dammegion Cymreig. Wrexham, 1862.

English Folk-heroes. Christina Hole. Batsford, 1948.

The Cambrian Journal. Vol. for 1859. Tenby.

The Cambrian Magazine. (Vol. i bound.) 1829.

The Cambrian Quarterly Magazine.

The Vale of Glamorgan: Scenes and Tales. Charles Redwood. London, 1839.

Tales & Sketches of Wales. Charles Wilkins. Cardiff, 1880.

Y Cymmrodor. The Journal of the Society of the Cymmrodorion. London.

Hanes Plwyf Defynog. D. Craianog Lewis. Merthyr, 1911.

Beddgelert, its Facts, Fairies & Folk-lore. D. E. Jenkins. Porthmadoc, 1899.

BIBLIOGRAPHY

Y Ficer Pritchard. D. Gwenallt Jones. Caernarfon.

Siluriana. D. Lloyd Isaac. Newport, 1859.

Ysten Sioned. D. Silvan Evans and John Jones. (2nd edn.) Wrexham, 1894.

Cyfaill yr Aelwyd a'r Frythones. Edited by Elfed and Cadrawd—began publication in 1892.

The Mythology and Rites of the British Druids. Edward Davies. London, 1809.

Folklore of the British Isles. Eleanor Hull. Methuen, 1928.

Coelion Cymru. Evan Isaac. Aberystwyth, 1938.

A Relation of the Apparitions of Spirits in . . . Wales. Edmund Jones. Trevecca, 1780.

Welsh Folk-lore. A Collection of the Folk-tales and Legends of North Wales. Elias Owen. Oswestry and Wrexham, 1896.

Welsh Sketches. 3rd series. London, 1854.

The Science of Fairy Tales: an enquiry into Fairy Mythology. Edwin Sidney Hartland. Methuen, 1925.

Recollections and Anecdotes of Edward Williams. Elijah Waring. London, 1850.

Tir Iarll. Frederic Evans. Cardiff, 1912.

Shakespeare & the Welsh. F. J. Harries. London, 1919.

The Lakes of Wales. Frank Ward. Herbert Jenkins, 1931.

The Itinerary through Wales. Giraldus Cambrensis. Dent, 1912.

BIBLIOGRAPHY

Chwedlau Dau Fynydd. G. M. Roberts. Llandebie, 1948.

English Legends. Henry Bett. Batsford, 1952.

Hynafiaethau Llandegai a Llanllechid. Hugh Derfel Hughes. Bethesda, 1866.

Y Tylwyth Teg. Hugh Evans. Liverpool, 1935.

Lectures [The Hibbert, 1886] *on the Origin & Growth of Religion as illustrated by Celtic Heathendom.* John Rhys.

The Golden Bough: A Study in Magic and Religion. J. G. Frazer. Abridged Edition, Macmillan, 1924.

Iolo MSS.: A Selection of Ancient Welsh Manuscripts. Llandovery, 1848.

Welsh Folk-lore of West and Mid-Wales. Jonathan Ceredig Davies. Aberystwyth, 1911.

Celtic Folklore, Welsh and Manx. John Rhys. (2 vols.) Oxford, 1901.

The Hero. Lord Raglan. Watts & Co. London.

Hanes Plwyfi Llangeler a Phenboyr. Daniel E. Jones. Llandyssul, 1899.

'*Slawer Dydd.* Llewelyn Williams. Llanelli, 1918.

Llyfr Gwybodaeth Gyffredinol. Sec. series. (The pagination is somewhat confusing; this applies also to one or two other bound volumes of old magazines.)

The Myvyrian Archaiology of Wales. Denbigh, 1870.

The Mabinogion. Lady Charlotte Guest. Dent.

Llên Gwerin Sir Gaernarfon. John Jones (*Myrddin Fardd*). Caernarfon, 1908.

BIBLIOGRAPHY

Folk-lore and Folk-Stories of Wales. Marie Trevelyan. London, 1909.

Wales. Owen M. Edwards. T. Fisher Unwin, 1901.

The Cambrian Popular Antiquities. 1815. Published in London by the Rev. Peter Roberts, A.M.

Storiau Gwallter Map. R. T. Jenkins. Llandebie, 1941.

Chwedlau Cefn Gwlad. Sarnicol. Aberystwyth, 1944.

A Book of Folk-lore. S. Baring Gould.

The History and Antiquities of the County of Cardigan. Samuel Rush Meyrick. London, 1808.

Transactions of the Honourable Society of Cymmrodorion.

A Topographical Dictionary of Wales. (3rd edn.) London, 1843.

Welsh Folklore and Folk-Custom. T. Gwynn Jones. Methuen, 1930.

History of Brecknock. Theophilus Jones. (Glanusk edition.)

The Works of Thomas Love Peacock. (Vol. ii. *The Misfortunes of Elphin*). London, Richard Bentley & Son, 1875.

Tours in Wales. Thomas Pennant, edited by John Rhys (3 vols.). Caernarvon, 1883.

Myths and Legends of the Celtic Race. T. W. Rolleston. Harrap, London. (2nd edn.)

Radnorshire in History, Topography & Romance. William Bowen Hamer. Llandrindod Wells, 1914.

Cambrian Superstitions. W. Howells. Tipton, 1831.

BIBLIOGRAPHY

Hanes Plwyf Llandyssul. W. J. Davies. Llandyssul, 1896.

Lives of the Cambro-British Saints. W. J. Rees. Llandovery, 1853.

De Nugis Curialium. Cymmrodorion Record Series No. ix. 1923.

British Goblins—Welsh Folk-lore, Fairy Mythology, Legends and Traditions. Wirt Sikes. London, 1880.

Y Brython. Cylchgrawn Llenyddol Cymru. (Bound in four volumes.) Tremadog. 1858–63.

Y Wladva Gymreig. L. J. Caernarvon. 1898.

Siaced Fraith. Elizabeth Williams. Gwasg Aberystwyth. 1952.